BARBED
WIRE

BARBED WIRE

ELIZABETH FACKLER

St. Martin's Press
New York

Design by Jessica Winer

Library of Congress Cataloging-in-Publication Data

Fackler, Elizabeth.
  Barbed Wire.

    I. Title.
PS3556.A28B37 1986   813'.54   86-13476
ISBN 0-312-06640-6

First Edition

10 9 8 7 6 5 4 3 2 1

To Mabel Marion

BARBED WIRE

1

People joke about Texas weather, but if you've ever lived there you know it's not funny. We're talking a hundred and six in the shade and the wind feels like it's blown through a fissure from the core of a volcano. It's enough to knock you over, that wind, enough to topple you from whatever balance you may have attained.

When I first came to Dallas I was often off balance. For instance, I'd thought Texas was part of the Great Southwest and everyone would walk around inside these terrific tans. Instead everyone walks around inside air-conditioned buildings. When they have to leave they make a run for their air-conditioned cars. They work out in refrigerated gyms and drink in dark caverns reminiscent of the ice age. I was cold a lot in Texas, shivering in that artificial chill after coming in drenched from the heat outside. I didn't have an air-conditioned car, being one of the Yankee masses that had come to Texas for a job, bringing our old cars, bought where air-conditioning wasn't necessary for survival.

I learned a lot about survival that year. Learned it through the death of a good friend in the same way you learn about a fishhook by running your finger toward the point. A quick, sharp pain tells you the point isn't the weapon—the weapon is a barb hidden beneath the edge.

It was one of those oven days when I unwittingly left Dallas for the last time and pulled into Austin in the late afternoon. I had a headache from the heat and the six-pack of Lone Star I'd consumed on the drive down. It's legal to drink beer while driving in Texas, a luxury they pay for in gory highway statistics. I missed that ignominious fate and coasted into the underground garage of my hotel with only a throbbing head to pay for my sin.

The concrete dust of the garage felt cool and I let its coolness settle over me for a minute after I turned off the engine. Then I collected my stuff and zombied up to the lobby. I bought a paper without even looking at it, let alone suspecting that the news it contained would change my life. Declining the bellboy's help and tip, I found the room myself and maneuvered my load far enough to dump it on the bed. I would have liked to curl up around my possessions and lose myself in oblivion but my clothes were soggy and I started shivering in the arctic air. So I made a beeline for the shower, marveling at how all the way from Dallas I'd anticipated a cool bath and now wanted the hot water blasting.

The view from my window was of the state capitol dwarfed by construction cranes and those high-rise glass tombs of modern architecture. Far below, a dry creekbed meandered its native thicket of insects and reptiles through the jungle of commerce as if to remind everyone that underneath the gloss and patina, nature lay in wait. The shower had revived me so I felt restless and ready to prowl Sixth Street for any stray female but, being a hooked journalist, I found the paper and spread it open on the still pristine bed. Scanning the headlines, my eye stopped at a small square story about a local suicide.

I knew her. She was in fact the only good thing that had happened to me in Austin, the only sugar in the bait that had drawn me there. I read the story two or three times, growing angry at the scant information. They called her Caroline Walbridge but I knew it was Arly. The age was right, and she lived in Holler.

Without even thinking I picked up the phone and punched in her number. It rang a long time. That's a lonely feeling, listening to a phone ringing in the home of someone no longer alive. And then I thought if I'd called her yesterday maybe she would be. I hadn't because I'd wanted to surprise her, wanted to listen to the pleasure ripple through her laugh. I felt let down that she was gone, but I also felt like a buffoon that she'd needed someone and I hadn't known.

I could've called yesterday, last week, any time in the last three months. I hadn't because I hadn't thought she'd needed me. Well, that was at least part of the reason. Arly had always seemed up to me, handling things, in control. She seemed to like her distance as much as I like mine. She was one of those true friends you could call up when you hit town, get together and party with for a few days. Then it was time's up, gotta go, give me a kiss for the road. But she wasn't just a party girl; there was more, a deeper current of understanding, a sympathy that surged in silence behind the jokes and good times.

I liked her, I really did. And the quality I admired most was her spirit. She had fight every inch of her spine. So what had happened in three months? From the messages I'd picked up last time I'd seen her, not just from her words but from her quick smile, her easy posture—God, her every movement was in harmony: she wasn't even close to falling apart.

I went out for another six-pack and as an afterthought picked up a plate of nachos. Waiting for the cheese to melt in the microwave behind the bar, I watched the people, listened to their drawled words and the soft crescendo of their laughter, my mind filled with gloomy thoughts that Arly was better than any of them, more vital, more responsive to the things that really mattered, and yet she was dead while they guffawed at dirty jokes. The afternoon paper was on the bar and I found the story and read it again, letting the greasy cheese drip on the newsprint. I looked up to see the bartender watching me and I slid the story toward him.

"I knew her," I said, needing to tell someone.

His eyes squinted to read the headline upside down. "It's a tough world," he murmured in sympathy.

I grunted and took my package beer and left. Yeah it was, but Arly was tough. Of all the women I'd known, I thought she could take it.

Back in my room I watched the evening news in hopes of catching something about her, but it was all about the legislature opening tomorrow—my assignment and ostensibly my reason for coming to Austin. But the real reason, the reason I'd wanted to come, was to see Arly. I finished my beer and crawled sodden into bed. The drapes shut out all light and the darkness was in turmoil from the cold air storming above the sheet where I lay naked, limp and helpless. I wanted to grieve for Arly but I couldn't really believe it. Maybe I needed to see her buried for that.

I got back up and turned on a light, found the paper and read the story again. No mention of the funeral. Maybe it would be private. A suicide, after all. In the darkness again I tried to picture Arly putting a noose around her neck and jumping off. I couldn't. Someone had done it to her and I didn't mean driven her to it. Someone had put that rope on and pushed her. It was as evident to me as if I'd seen it happen.

The next morning I didn't go to the opening of the legislature but drove east out of the city toward Holler. The choppy hills of Austin level off pretty fast going east. The land is swept by mammoth rounded plains, each one disappearing into the crevice of the beginning of another. The trees are sparse, most of them fringing plowed fields, blackland clay turning hard and shiny like peeled rubber in the sun. But in thirty miles the pines begin, scattered outcrop-

4

pings at first, then the road is winding through a sunlight speckled forest so thick you'd need a machete to walk through it.

Arly had told me how to get to her place once. I'd been half-listening, but I remembered the turning left by the water tower just before the curve into Holler. The road looked more like a farmer's lane but, what the hell, this was Texas. My Celica had seen better days and I took the crusted ruts slow and easy, following the edge of fields a good mile and a half off the highway. Back under the trees the road forked and there was a country store with a squat, faded mailbox next to a pay phone. I stopped to use the phone.

I knew the number by heart but it didn't help, there was no answer. The store, Decker's, was closed. There was a black wreath on the door.

I went back to Austin and sat in on the legislature. I didn't hear a word, wasn't even aware what the issue was. I just sat there in that mahogany gallery, staring at the antique lamps whose covered bulbs redundantly spell out Texas over the heirs of Sam Houston and Davy Crockett. The natural environment of Texas is unlivable in my opinion, and how the pioneers made it without even ice cubes is beyond me. They're tough people, the descendents of the pioneers. They don't hang themselves.

2

It was three days before I gathered my courage to try again. I don't know what took me so long. Maybe I just couldn't face her funeral and wanted to allow plenty of time for it to be over. Or maybe somehow I knew in my gut what a hornets' nest I was walking into and my better judgment succeeded in stalling me. Or hell, it might've just been the heat. When I slowed to make the turn by the water tower, the humidity crowded my car like a fat hitchhiker. The tower was a relic from the days before the dam, when Holler was a patch of nothing. When they started mining sulfur around the other side of town, they needed water, and lo and behold the Nunca River was dammed and a reservoir created. Now tourism vied with the mine for magnetic pull.

Arly had grown up here. She'd fought the mine balls-to-the-wall over environmental issues, even landed in jail a few times for disrupting the flow of business. There's a legend about the Yellow Rose of Texas. Yeah, I know the song; but there's some historical veracity here in that a mulatto beauty preoccupied Santa Ana while the Texans pussyfooted in for their surprise attack. This all happened at San Jacinto, their Yorktown. So if you call someone a Yellow Rose, you're saying she's acting with the best interest of Texas at heart. Arly had done that for most of her life. And then she'd stopped doing it.

She'd never talked about giving it up and I didn't pry. When she was with me, she was a woman enjoying herself. There were no obsessions, no brooding gaps of resolution. And if she'd dropped organizing rather abruptly, it hadn't shown any scars. She'd probably just outgrown it. She was in transition and that was part of what bothered me so much. I'd looked forward to seeing her again, and not just to share more good times. I wanted to see where she'd land next.

There was a local yokel standing in front of Decker's store so I pulled up to ask directions. He was mid-thirties, blond and washed-out looking, his demeanor a contradictory blend of swagger and subservience. I wiped the sweat off my forehead and asked if he knew the way to Arly's trailer.

"Yeah, sure," he drawled, a sick smile curling his lips, "but she ain't there."

I looked at him hard, digging for his gut reaction. It was too camouflaged by his posturing, his constant shuffling between hooking his thumbs in his belt and sliding them into his back pockets, safe and out of sight. "I'm a friend of the family," I finally said.

He snorted but gave me vague directions and then looked at the ground. I felt like tipping him, but didn't.

I followed his directions—about a mile down, hidden behind a row of pines—and parked next to a yellow Camaro, inwardly groaning. In my opinion, women who own yellow cars are the most melancholy chicks going. Especially if it has a black interior. If it's got a black interior, watch out—that woman is going to have you wishing you weren't born before the night's reached its sad, lonely climax.

I was at a disadvantage not knowing her name and felt awkward crossing the yard to the closed up trailer. The air conditioner hummed beneath the eerie cry of grackles and the hacksaw rasp of locust. Even in the shade by the door, I felt overwhelmed by the humidity and thought surely she would let me in. After all, it was a pioneer tradition to take a stranger in out of the elements.

I knocked and looked around Arly's yard. You could see the river in a lacy pattern behind the trees. The lawn was spacious and had originally been carefully defined but was now overgrown with tall, coarse grass and stalky clumps of darkeyed susans. There was a path from the door to a redwood picnic table under the trees. A tire swing hung motionless from one of the big oaks. The whole place looked low-class homey. Not to be disparaging, but the kind of comforts people who never had money would think pretty nice.

The door opened and the new tenant of Arly's trailer stood disguised behind the shimmer of screen. I let her get a good look at me and then said, "Frank James. I called you earlier."

"You just missed Mrs. Walbridge," she answered quickly, making no move to open the door.

I looked down the driveway Arly's mother had used to escape, sorry I had missed her by so little. "Didn't see her," I said, looking back at the shadowed outline of a woman behind the glossy screen. It was impossible to talk to her, hidden as she was. She could see me clearly but all I got were glimmering flashes that never congealed into a whole impression. So I pulled the old ploy and asked for a drink of water.

She turned into an obliging hostess, flipped the lock on the screen and said pleasantly, "Sure. Come on in."

I stepped gratefully into the cold brace of winter and closed the door. She was slender, tall, wearing baggy jeans and a grungy T-shirt. Her hair was black and heavy, straight to her shoulders, cutting a diagonal across her pale clean cheek. When she handed me the glass, there was

8

something in her dark eyes, the way she veiled them behind her fan of lashes, and how she was careful our fingers didn't touch, that made me pin her for a virgin. I thanked her and sipped the icy water.

"This is all Arly's stuff," she said. "I rented the place as is."

The room was a jumble of open boxes, emptied drawers, brimming wastepaper baskets. "She wasn't very neat," I said.

"Oh, she didn't leave it like this." She piled things off the benches onto the floor, clearing a space at the table. "Come sit down," she said. "All this is from Mrs. Walbridge. She went through Arly's things and took what she wanted. I'm supposed to take care of the rest."

"She was pretty quick renting the place out," I ventured.

"Arly was supporting her, she needs the money."

"Oh." I sat down in my oasis, feeling doubly for the old lady. "So you're just cleaning up for her," I fumbled, to keep going.

"No, I rented it. I'm sorry, I haven't told you my name. I'm Baxter McCullough."

"Baxter?" I couldn't help asking.

"A family name."

I nodded dumbly.

"So what did you want to see of Arly's?" she prodded, helping me. "Was it something specific?"

"It doesn't make sense to me," I answered. "I guess I'm just looking for something to make it real." I picked a photo of Arly and a man from a box at my elbow. "Who is this with her?"

"Chad Eby. Her boyfriend, or at least her main one. From what I gather, she was pretty popular."

Eby was tall, pencil-thin, and blond. He had hard good looks that bordered on snide, but photographs can lie. His arm was across Arly's shoulder and you could see her hand

9

coming around his waist. She was barefoot, wearing cutoffs and a T-shirt without a bra. Her sunny face was open, her energy and confidence shining out of her, making Eby look like a poser, or the escort of a star. If you were to look at that picture and pick out the person likely to commit suicide, it wouldn't be Arly. I put the photo back and stood up.

The things of hers that showed through the rubble were from nature. Bouquets of dried grasses tied to the walls, a blown-up poster of a coyote howling at the moon, driftwood, a painted cow's skull, a stretched rattlesnake skin inside a glass case above the door. There was a pine hat rack screwed into the wall, empty. "I just wish I could bring it home," I muttered.

"Did you go to the funeral?" Baxter asked from behind me.

I shook my head.

"That's what they're for," she said gently.

"Maybe that's why not," I said, turning around. "When I can believe it, then I'll bury Arly in my mind."

She looked puzzled. "Do you think it wasn't Arly?"

I stared down the hall. "Can I go in there?" I kept my voice soft, knowing I would look around no matter what she said.

She nodded, still puzzled but suspending judgment; I gave her credit for that. The whole left wall of the trailer was closed doors. I opened one and found it crammed with hiking gear, fishing rods, roller skates. A frisbee fell out and I slid it back in carefully and closed the door. To the right was the bath, minuscule and mildewed, and beyond it was the bedroom. A pair of those twelve-foot-long horns was mounted over her bed. I smiled at them, and I sorely missed never having spent a night with Arly here in her domain. The place reeked of her, her independence, her strength, her courage damn it. I went back to the front more affirmed in my doubt.

"So what did you find?" she asked when I was sitting across from her again.

I shook my head, trying to loose the cobwebs of melancholy that were tangling in my mind. "Don't you find it strange, being here in her house?"

She shrugged. "I didn't know her. Besides, it's cheap and I'm short on funds. It's stocked with everything I need and I'm doing Mrs. Walbridge a favor by taking care of it for her. I don't believe in ghosts, if that's what you mean."

"No bad vibes? Psychic repercussions?"

"I haven't felt any."

I didn't either. The place had a deathly stillness. "Do you know where she did it?"

Her eyes flashed real wide and then she smiled a benevolent pardon. "We all have a ghoulish curiosity, don't we? I wanted to see it too."

The heat hit us in the face as we left the trailer and I couldn't keep myself from hoping it wasn't far. We walked through a tabernacle choir of locusts and then along the edge of the river on a ragged rocky beach. The water was narrow here, a hundred yards across maybe. We took a path away from it, a steep climb up a limestone cliff, and then we were in a meadow of large trees. I tried to pick one out that looked likely or showed scars, but they were all the same to me, none different from the others. We were in the sun now and Baxter kept a direct course for shade. We stopped under a cottonwood and she pointed at the branch above our heads.

"This is it," she said.

My reaction was immediate. "It's too high. How could she reach it?"

"They found her shoe in the tree. Apparently she climbed up and jumped."

"I don't believe it," I said.

"What do you mean?"

The locusts were rasping all around us. I could feel sweat running down the small of my back. "Someone did it to her."

"Murder?" she whispered, and her dark eyes flared.

"I shouldn't have told you." I felt sorry to have frightened her.

She shook her head, her hair bouncing against those pale cheeks. "What makes you think it wasn't suicide?"

"I just don't believe it."

"A lot of people have that problem with death."

"I know death. I can't accept Arly killing herself."

"Haven't you ever wanted to do it?"

I considered briefly. "No. And neither did she."

"You're sure?" There was disbelief in her voice.

I nodded.

"That's all you have to go on?"

"So far."

She studied me a moment. "What are you going to do?"

"Let's go back to the trailer," I suggested, taking her elbow. She came along, didn't shy away or go all stiff like I expected her to. Maybe she wasn't a virgin after all. I felt ashamed to be thinking about getting laid while I was trying to figure this all out, but I reasoned that Arly, of all people, would understand.

3

Back in the trailer, I felt like a polar bear in his element. Baxter came through and offered me a beer. I accepted and sank into my former seat, watching her take two bottles of Bud from the refrigerator and open them on one of those gadgets under the lip of the counter. I'd noticed a Midwestern twang in her speech, subdued as if she'd gone to a good college, so I knew she wasn't a native. "Where you from?" I asked as she handed me the beer.

"Chicago," she answered, confirming my guess that she was from my neck of the woods, relatively speaking.

"What brought you to Texas?"

She hesitated just a second, looking embarrassed. "I came to write a book."

A fellow writer. "About Texas?"

She shook her head. "It's journals, really, some I kept over the last several years. I'm going to condense them into one volume."

"What are they about?" I asked politely, remembering the yellow car with black interior.

She shrugged. "My analysis."

I laughed. "What ever brought you here to do that?"

She laughed too, an easy, sensuous sound. "It seemed far away."

My own motive hadn't been much different. I thought of spending a pleasant afternoon exploring what else Baxter and I had in common but when I looked around, the reality of Arly hit me again. The last thing I wanted was to face the heat outside, but there were answers I needed that weren't to be found in comfort. I asked if I could come back when I was done in town. She studied me with her dark eyes and I've never felt so uneasy under a scrutiny before. But evidently she liked what she saw because she said yes.

Holler was a false-front main street facing the railroad tracks and two side streets of modern stores. The police station was a new brick building, a little too imposing for the size of the town. I followed the arrows up one side of a pair of curving stairs to the second floor and found myself in an antebellum-width hallway with offices on both sides. At the end of the polished linoleum was Sheriff Pickles Offut's office.

I caught Offut teasing his secretary. He was sitting on the corner of her desk with his back to the door when I came in. She was blushing and had her hands primly rigid in her lap. Offut laughed when he heard the door, slapped the desk and stood up to greet me. His secretary jumped as his palm hit the wood, then turned embarrassed eyes to me, imploring that I forget what I'd seen.

I introduced myself as a reporter for the Dallas *Spur*. Offut was impressed and took me into his office, shut the door, and sat down behind his desk. He was a big man, had probably played football when he was young, but he was well over forty now and more beefy than solid. He had short curly brown hair and a round face with pink fleshy cheeks laced with veins. His smile, showing small even teeth, seemed to corral a habitual growl.

"What can I do for you, Mr. James?" he asked, leaning back and regarding me from his official platform.

"We're doing a feature on suicides," I said. "There's been a dramatic increase in them lately and we're investigating the ones we hear about. I'm interested in the Walbridge case."

He didn't blink an eye. "What do you want to know?"

"What made the coroner call it suicide?"

His eyes narrowed. "She hung herself."

I pulled a notepad out of my pocket and began to doodle. "There was a chair and a note and everything?"

"No chair. We found one of her shoes in the tree. She climbed up there, tied the rope to a branch, and jumped off."

"Was there a note?"

He looked at me a long time before answering. "There's the privacy of the family to consider," he finally said. "I wouldn't want you bothering Mrs. Walbridge."

I smiled as humbly as I could. "That's why I'm here talking to you, sir."

"It's all public record," he stalled. "You can look it up downstairs."

"Why don't you tell me."

He sat up straighter and folded his arms on the desk. "There was a note," he conceded.

"How did you know she wrote it?"

"It was done on her typewriter. We had that checked by an expert."

"Did she sign it?"

"No, she didn't. But we dusted the keys and found only her prints."

"You checked it all pretty thoroughly, Sheriff."

"We try to be careful," he said, settling back again and regarding me with suspicion.

"What was the motive?" I asked quietly.

"It's in the coroner's report. If you reporters would do your homework you wouldn't have to ask so many questions."

15

He seemed awfully touchy. "Why don't you just tell me what it said."

"I'm not telling you anything you couldn't read yourself right downstairs," he barked. "She was pregnant. That's why she did it."

He couldn't have surprised me more if he'd punched me in the gut. "How far along?" I asked coldly.

"Two months," the sheriff said, amused at my reaction. "Just enough time to realize she'd gotten caught and be ashamed of herself."

I stared in disbelief. "Ashamed of being pregnant?"

He leaned back in his chair and sighed. "You're not from Texas, are you, Mr. James?"

"I live in Dallas," I answered tersely. "Are you saying Arly killed herself because she was pregnant?"

His eyes shone with glee that I'd cracked my cover. "If you knew Miss Walbridge, you know she came from an old family hereabouts. They never had much money, but they've always been good churchgoing people . . . until she came along. She shamed her family more than once, and I guess even she knew when she'd gone too far."

His logic was numbing. "Sheriff," I said, struggling to conclude the interview, "is there any possibility it wasn't suicide?"

He sat still, his eyes boring into me. "You reporters are all dirty whores, scrounging around stirring up scandal where there ain't none. Arly Walbridge was a bullshit environmentalist. By the time you get through with her she'll be the assassinated leader of a feminist army." He stood up and squared his shoulders with the full authority of his office. "This is just a sordid little suicide in small town Texas, mister. Leave it be."

There was something more than righteousness behind his eyes. There was a touch of fear, an effort at intimidation.

I thanked him for his time and left. His secretary wasn't at her desk, and I walked out into the hall feeling more baffled than when I went in. Arly being pregnant was no answer to anything but it opened up a lot of questions. The obvious one being who was the father? Two months meant it wasn't mine and that was a relief. Just because I don't want kids doesn't mean I want them to die. Arly's kid died with her. Arly's and whose?

I met Offut's secretary on the stairs. She was well built, with a blouse cut low enough to show a good cleavage. No wonder Offut bothered her, the way she threw everything she had right in your face. She stopped in front of me, blocking my descent.

"You're new in town, aren't you?" she asked, her lips freshly coated with purple gloss.

I introduced myself.

"Teresa Wains," she said without being asked. "You won't say nuthin' about what you saw, will you?"

I shook my head, having no inclination toward town-hall gossip.

"It don't mean nuthin', really. He just gets randy when he's bored."

"Is he like that with everyone, then?"

She giggled. "It's disgustin' but what're you gonna do? I'll bet there's not a woman in Holler who hasn't felt the long arm of the law up her dress."

I grunted, not amused. "Well, then, your reputation would be sullied if he left you alone," I said sarcastically.

"Hey, that's right," she chimed, reaching out a heavily baubled hand to touch my arm. But I was gone, past her grip, hurrying down the stairs without a backward glance.

I came out of the building into a furnace blast of blinding heat. My Celica was parked in full sun and I had to force myself into it. The traffic was all people air-conditioned behind closed windows. Even the trucks had air-conditioning. I saw a poor sucker ahead walking and felt sorry for him. And then I recognized him as Chad Eby. Pulling to a stop alongside the curb, I called his name.

17

4

The photograph had flattered him. He was borderline handsome but there was a hardness in the jutting bones of his face that gave him a mean edge. He scrutinized me from the sizzling sidewalk as if he was comfortable squinting off the glare of concrete in the hundred and six degree sun.

"I was a friend of Arly's," I said softly to coax him closer.

He squatted by the passenger door and leaned his arms on the open window, his hands aggressively dangling over the seat. He was looking me over and I don't think he especially liked what he saw. But I figured he felt as I did—preoccupied with the goodness of Arly and jealous of someone who may have stolen what had turned out to be precious hours. "I'd like to talk to you," I suggested. "Is there someplace we could get a drink?"

He assessed me a moment longer and then said easily, "Yeah, sure, man, we can go to my club." He opened the door and slid in, folding his long legs so his knees stuck up in front of the dash.

Holler was in a half-dry county and the natives joined a club if they wanted to drink hard liquor. Chad's was a nice one, a huge room scattered with sofas and overstuffed chairs, mammoth rock fireplace and picture windows overlooking the Nunca River. We settled into opposite loveseats and stared at each other until the waitress came. Chad gave her the coupons he'd bought at the desk, forcing me to be his guest, and watched her ass as she walked away. Then he turned back to me, his arms spread along the back of the couch, and asked, "So where did you know Arly from?"

"I met her in Austin," I answered.

"When?"

"About a year ago."

"She never mentioned you."

"I didn't see her often."

"Just blow into town, eat at the local diner and then back on the route, eh? Selling those brushes? Making that quota?"

"I'm a reporter," I said.

"No kidding," he said, and smiled at the waitress coming with our drinks. "Hey Holly," he said to her, almost under his breath, "you save time for me tonight?"

"I always got time for you, sugar." She smiled like she meant it, but walked away without their naming an assignation.

"So what do *you* do?" I asked, not bothering to hide my amusement at his little game.

"Nothing," he said. "I'm a bum."

"Rich kid, huh?"

He shook his head. "I used to be a musician."

"What happened?"

"Nothing." He laughed and I found myself liking him. He was hard, there was an edge, but he had a spontaneity, an ability to laugh at himself, that was infectious. I could see why Arly liked him and that made me feel a whole lot better.

"I saw that photo of you and Arly she had. You looked good together."

"Yeah? Where'd you see it?"

"At her place."

He sipped his drink, watching me as he considered. "What're you looking for?"

"Does it make sense to you?"

"What?"

"Arly."

"Nah. Hell, what does?"

"Did you know she was pregnant?"

He looked at me hard for just an instant and then visibly relaxed his body and drawled, "Who told you that?"

"Offut."

His eyes shot fast to mine again. Then he gave up, crumpled back against the sofa and looked at the ceiling. "Jesus," he said, looking at me again, "I had no idea."

"Was it yours?"

He took a quick swig of his whiskey and shrugged. "Could have been. Arly wasn't monogamous."

"Who else's might it be?"

"What about yours?" he asked, leaning back but not relinquishing his drink.

I shook my head. "Offut said two months. It's been three since I've seen her."

"Lucky you," he said, deadpan.

"It clears me as far as having a motive."

His gray eyes watched me now with the intensity of a predator. "Motive for what?"

"Murder," I said.

Holly came back to check on us but he waved her away without taking his eyes off me. When she was a safe distance away he whispered, "Did Offut say that?"

I shook my head.

He didn't relax at all; he stayed rigidly attentive. "So this is your theory?"

"Fact," I said.

"You got any proof?"

"No, but it's out there. I'll find it."

Only then did he lean back and seem to relax. He sipped his drink a few times, keeping his eyes on the table, holding his own counsel. When he looked at me again he almost smiled but lost it in a sickened grimace. "I told myself that suicide is always a shock, that the people left behind never understand. I kept telling myself that. But I didn't believe it. She wasn't the type. I kept coming back to that. Maybe, maybe everything else, but not Arly."

"Did you talk to the sheriff?"

"Huh!" he exclaimed. "I stay clear of him. You should talk to her mother. She doesn't believe it either."

"Are there very many people who don't believe it?"

He shrugged. "Who knows? Arly had a lot of friends. I suppose some of them are having trouble accepting it. But she's gone, you know. That's the real shocker. An official bureau puts a label on it and maybe you think about it, but the label isn't the big thing."

"Even if it's wrong?"

"Well, if it's wrong," he answered, as if thinking aloud but watching me warily, "then there's justice to be done. I'll bet you're the Lone Ranger, come to right our wrongs and leave us with a silver bullet in our heart."

"Why do you say that?" I asked, wincing.

"This town is a delicately balanced scaffold of power. If you try to insert instant justice you'll topple the whole thing, and then what'll we have? The toughs, the bullies, the headcrunchers in power. Leave it be, James. You'll only make things worse."

"Why will an inquiry into Arly's death topple the power structure?"

His eyes were shiny and closed. "I've said my piece." He stood, excusing himself to another appointment, telling me I was welcome to stay as long as I wished and then leaving me without any coupons.

But I was saved because Holly came back and said Chad had put my tab on his bill. I was curious why he would do that but ordered another whiskey anyway. When Holly brought it, I asked her to sit down.

"Oh, we're not allowed," she answered instantly, and then looked at me as if she was sorry.

I remembered her banter with Eby. "Can I ask you a few questions?"

She shrugged. "Sure, I guess. Are you a credit investigator or something?"

"What makes you ask that?"

"Well, you were talking to Chad, and he left kind of huffy."

"Are his finances shaky?"

She narrowed her heavily mascara-ed eyes. "You were just talking to him."

"Did you know Arly Walbridge?"

She changed from a hard-as-nails bargirl to the kid next door. "Yeah, I did," she said, "we used to be real close."

"Kind of a shock, what happened."

"Was it ever. Blew me away. I mean Arly, of all people."

"Did you ever think it wasn't true?"

She paled, laughed hoarsely and looked frightened. "Is this a joke? I was at her funeral."

"I mean about the suicide part."

I could tell she knew the answer before she asked, "What else could it be?"

"Murder."

"Oh my God," she whispered, sinking down to sit on the low, glass table in front of me. She seemed bewildered a moment, and then she looked at me and there was triumph in her eyes. "I'd sooner believe that than suicide. But who would do it? Who hated her that much?"

"Who hated her at all?"

"Oh, well, Arly was strong, you know? She rubbed a lot of people the wrong way."

"Like who, especially?"

She remembered herself suddenly and stood up, leaning to dust the table with her rag. "We had a falling out a few years ago. I really don't know that much about what was happening in her life. Why don't you talk to her mother?" And then without a backward glance she walked away, around the corner and out of sight.

5

Everyone wanted me to see Mrs. Walbridge. First Baxter, and then Sheriff Pickles Offut had underhandedly steered me in that direction. Chad Eby had practically ordered it, and Holly the barmaid had offered it as a friendly suggestion. Sometimes I go against the flow just to be ornery, but the heat that flattened my senses as soon as I stepped outside the club was influential. I made a beeline back to Baxter's trailer.

I used to think high noon was the hottest part of the day, but it isn't. The heat is at its most intense in the long hours of the afternoon, when you're begging for dusk or even just a breath of air. It was four o'clock, square in the middle of that natural impasse, when the heat and the rotation of the earth stare each other down and it's not at all clear which will win. If it weren't for the laws of probability, you would bet on the heat winning hands down and gloating about it forever. I studied the shadows of the trees for evidence of their lengthening as I eased past the row of trailer homes, all humming with their artificial comfort, which at that moment I desired more than the companionship of the woman who inhabited Arly's chilled container.

Baxter wasn't home. I couldn't believe it. I knocked a long time and even went to the back door and knocked a long time again. No answer. I stood there, unable to face that sun again. I had just about decided to wait in the merely stifling shade when I thought to visit the neighbor. The trailer was a faded, rusting yellow with a lot of flowers in beds beneath the surrounding trees. There was a swing, this one a board and two ropes, well-worn, and an old aluminum kitchen table with matching, torn chairs under a giant tree. I took all this in as I walked through the trees from Arly's place and into their yard. The driveway had been gravel once but was mostly dirt now, soft and powdery from the long drought. I remembered loving to squiggle my toes in silken dust like that when I was a kid. That was in farm country though, the Midwest. This was Texas. There was probably a hive of fire ants lurking just below the surface.

She answered the door so quickly I guessed she'd seen me coming. I could hear the TV on, a soap opera, and a baby making fussing noises. She was tiny, even standing above me. Her auburn hair was fine and wispy, falling well past her waist. She wore it pulled back behind her ears and two locks had escaped and made like Fu Man Chu sideburns getting lost in the rest of her hair. Her skin was pale, with ghostly freckles, her lashes and brows almost invisible. She had blue eyes that were guarded but interested, a mouth that begged for attention.

I introduced myself as a friend of Arly's and asked if I could speak with her a bit. She listened and only blinked a few times, then said "Okay. Let me get the baby." I was left facing the closed door. I took a few steps away, bitterly disappointed that she hadn't chosen to share her air-conditioning with me.

She came out with a baby wrapped in a thin blanket and led me to the table nearby. She put the baby on the table, opening the blanket and revealing a can of Lone Star laying on its side. She set the kid on its stomach and turned

25

around, handing me the can. "I brought you a beer if you want it."

"You're not having one?" I asked, holding the cold can greedily.

She shook her head and sat down. "Why don't you sit?" she asked, gesturing toward the chair at the opposite end of the table. I did and opened the beer, took a long refreshing draught of it, and suppressed a burp as I smiled at her. "So, what's your name?" I began.

"Kerrie Hauper." She reached a hand out and jiggled the baby a little, as if afraid it would go to sleep and leave us alone.

"Did you know Arly well?"

She nodded, and this time when she blinked I saw tears brimming behind her flaxen lashes. "She was my best friend," she stated simply.

"I'm sorry," I said. "She was a good friend of mine, too. It was a real shock, what happened."

"I'll say."

"How did you hear about it?"

"I saw the police over there," she answered without hesitation, but her eyes wanted to know why I was asking.

"Did you talk to them?"

"'Course I did."

"What did they say? I mean, can you remember if they called it suicide right off?"

"I think so. I was pretty upset. I asked Ben Jackson, he's the deputy and he was kind of standin' guard, keepin' folks away. I asked him what happened and he said Arly hung herself in the cottonwood grove down by the river. Yeah, I remember now, that's what he said."

"And that's the first you heard about it being suicide?"

"That's the first I knew she was dead. I thought someone had burglared her trailer or somethin' and that's why the cops were there."

"Did she ever say anything, give any indication that she was thinking about killing herself?"

"No, she never. But she wasn't given to complainin', she was always the one to bolster up other people."

"So you believed it?"

She twitched her head, as if throwing her hair back off her eyes in a habitual gesture. "I don't know. That's what they said, so I s'pose it's true."

"Didn't it surprise you?"

"Don't it always, when people do somethin' like that?" She stood up and fussed with the baby's diaper, making him whimper under her whispered words. "Anyway, it's too late now."

"Too late for what?"

"To help her."

"What could you have done?"

"Jeepers, I don't know." She picked up the baby and held him close against her breasts. One of his tiny fists beat the air with futility.

"Did you ever think it wasn't true, that she didn't do it to herself?"

Her eyes got real wide, as if she knew what I was leading up to. "Arly wasn't stupid," she breathed, "it couldn't have been an accident."

I stood up too. "Could it have been murder?" I suggested very softly.

She stared at me, clutching the baby so close I thought she would smother him. "Who would do that?" she whispered.

"You tell me. You were her best friend."

She shifted the baby onto her hip. "Arly had a lot of friends. I gotta go start dinner."

"Just a minute more, Kerrie. Did she have any enemies?"

She shook her head. "I don't know. She went a lot of places, you know? I just saw her when she was home."

"Isn't there anyone she mentioned, anyone that bothered her more than the others?"

She looked away, down the drive, across the shrubbery to Arly's yard. "There was one she used to curse a lot," she said, so softly I could barely hear.

"Who was that?"

"What's gonna happen if I tell?" she asked, biting her lip.

I wanted to reassure her but I wanted to be honest too. I was a stranger out of nowhere and I knew the only way to get these people to trust me was to be straight with them. "I'm going to prove Arly was murdered, Kerrie. I need any help you can give me."

"I'll tell," she said, jerking the baby onto her other hip and casting a quick glance down the drive, "because what he did was wrong and it should come out. It was Pickles Offut. He used to push himself on her when she was just a kid, workin' in the church nursery. During the Sunday services, if that isn't the spit of the Devil. She told me how he'd come in with all those sleepin' babies and pin her up against the changin' table, holdin' his hand over her mouth the whole time."

"He raped her?" I asked, incredulous.

She nodded, her face flushed with embarrassment. "More'n once. She said he done it lots of times."

"Why didn't she blow the whistle on him?"

"Couldn't. He said he'd bust her boyfriend's pot field if she told. Said he'd go to jail forever and she'd never see him again."

"Who was that?"

"How Toffler. He and Arly went together in high school and a couple years after that. How grows marijuana on his daddy's farm. Least he used to."

"What's he do now?"

"He's in the county prison camp. Pickles busted him the day after Arly died."

"You sure about that?"

She nodded, and then the sound of a car hot-rodding up the road filled her face with terror. "I gotta go. You too. Quick now, my husband's awful jealous."

"Can I talk to you again?"

She was already hurrying toward the trailer. "Come earlier in the day," she threw back just before she disappeared behind the door.

I stepped into the bushes out of sight and watched a beat-up Trans Am pull in with a lot of noise. It was that guy who'd given me directions the first time I'd come out here. The one I'd felt like tipping because he'd been so subservient. I watched him jog confidently through the heat and disappear into the anonymous aluminum house. Then I walked back toward Arly's. Baxter's, I reminded myself.

6

So Pickles had raped Arly when she was just a kid, a teen-ager working in the church nursery. Probably it was her first lesson in the fallibility of authority, a lesson that had superseded the Christian doctrine of turning the other cheek, that had taught her the complexities of revenge against power. She had given herself who knows how many times to protect what she valued most in a teenager's lex-icon of values, her true love. But she hadn't submitted. Be-hind the sheriff's stifling hand had been born the mouth of a rebel.

It was a hard school; the lessons sunk in deep. Maybe it would have been better for her if she'd had some cowardice in her blood. If she'd run as far away from Holler as she could get, from the offending Pickles and the boy who'd accepted his freedom at the price of her debasement, she might still be alive. But she'd stayed to fight, to embroil herself in the sordid community that had formed her. Sometimes wisdom lies in admitting your weakness, in not tempting history to repeat itself.

I thought about Baxter, pulling her journals together into one final synopsis of her analysis. The end result of the pro-ject would be to crystallize the experience, the years of in-nuendos and shadows in mirrors, to freeze it all into the pages of one slim volume. It seemed dangerous to me, like going back for a snapshot of the dragon. Not that I thought she was shaky, but her illness had been pronounced over and she should be moving forward instead of looking back. That's what I like about journalism, the immediacy of it, the constant newness. It keeps you aware of the edge, and that's good. Because we're all on it, whether we watch our feet or not.

Baxter was on one for sure, living in a dead woman's home and trying to resurrect her own illness. I stood in the yard and watched Arly's trailer a while, watched the shadow woman flickering back and forth behind the curtains, thought about how much I would like to knock on that door and have Arly open it. Someone had stolen that from me. Someone had wrenched whole swatches from my life and left me with only reminders of a future that would never happen.

I had crossed the yard unthinkingly and now pounded loudly on the door. It opened as far as the chain would allow and a sliver of cold air knifed my face. "Oh it's you," Baxter said, closing the door then opening it wide. I stumbled into the refrigerated cubicle and sprawled unceremoniously on the couch.

She was standing at the door watching me. I looked around and saw that she'd cleared the place out, left only bare essentials and a few of the more impersonal decorations. She'd kept the wild weeds on the wall, but the rattlesnake was gone, along with the coyote. The black Puye pot was still there, beside a stack of books that were new. I looked back at Baxter. "You've been busy."

"Ummm," she said, still eyeing me warily.

I straightened up a little and, remembering the beer can in my hand, gestured to throw it away. "It's hot outside," I said unnecessarily.

She took care of the can and opened the refrigerator. "Want another?"

"Sure."

She gave me a Bud and poured herself a glass of lemonade. It looked good and she looked pretty, sipping the froth off the top of the ice floating in her glass. I remembered Arly doing that with margaritas, and how I liked to catch the tequila off her tongue before she'd swallowed all of it, how her lips would be tart with lime juice and then inside, beneath the icy drink, her mouth would be hot and inviting. She was the most vital woman I'd ever known, someone who seemed to have been born knowing how to live. Even Pickles Offut hadn't tainted her with his poison, even Holler, Texas, hadn't dampened her spirit. There was only one way to put Arly down and that was to kill her. Someone had done just that and it had to be someone stupid enough to think the world would believe it was suicide. It had to be someone conniving and sly but blind to the deeper textures of reality.

Baxter was watching me.

"Tell me what you saw," I said, rousing myself, "when you first came in here."

She took a step back to lean against the door, perusing the room from her original vantage point. She spoke slowly, remembering. "We came in the morning. The birds were noisy in the trees, lots of grackles with their eerie melancholy whistles. Mrs. Walbridge came in first and I followed her, standing here in the door, almost afraid to close it. It was hot from having been shut up and dark with the drapes all drawn. She turned on a lamp and then the air conditioner and said, real sad and tired sounding, 'Close the door, sweetie.' She wasn't crying but her face was full of pain. She waddled past me and disappeared in the other end of the trailer.

"I didn't follow her. I stood here and looked at the room as Arly had left it. Well, not exactly. The police had been here. They'd taken the typewriter and the note. There were crusted slivers of blackland clay from their feet on the floor.

A beer can was on the counter, nearly full. The paper on the couch was open to the movie section. A pair of running shoes lay by the door, as if she'd kicked them off when she came in and stuffed the socks into them. Her hat hung on the rack, a straw cowboy hat with feathers in the band.

"Mrs. Walbridge called for me to bring her a box and I went back into the bedroom. She'd emptied drawers onto the bed and was sorting through some papers, winnowing some into a small pile at the side. She asked me to put those into the box. They were letters mostly, a few legal looking documents, her car registration, things like that. She took her jewelry box without looking in it, a few pieces of clothing—a shawl, a scarf. Then she came out here and started going through drawers, quickly, as if she knew the contents, she just wanted a last look. She took a few photos and Arly's hat. That was all. Told me to keep what I wanted and put the rest in the yard."

"What happened to it then?"

"A man came with a truck and took them away."

A full can of beer and the paper opened to the movie section. Slivers of blackland clay. Running shoes by the door.

"Did you notice if her shoes had any clay on them?"

She thought a minute. "No, I don't think so. I mean I didn't notice then, but I packed them for Goodwill and I don't remember that they were especially dirty." She watched me a moment and then came away from the door, leaving her lemonade on the counter, to stand before me. "Frank, what proof do you really have that it wasn't suicide?"

I swallowed hard. "She was pregnant. That's what they give for the motive. Arly wouldn't kill herself because she was pregnant. She'd have an abortion maybe, but I even doubt that."

Baxter looked skeptical. She moved to stand in front of

the sink, staring into the darkness falling outside the window. I felt sorry that I was bringing her into this. But then I remembered that she was the one who had come here herself, and maybe there was something she needed here too.

"There's more," I said, leaning back and looking around the room. "You told me yourself. There was a full can of beer and the paper was open to the movies. Who opens a beer, looks to see what movies are in town, and then decides to kill herself instead?"

Baxter's face was perfectly still as she stared out the window.

"Somebody came to that door," I said softly, "maybe she was opening the beer and someone knocked, she set the beer down, opened the door, and let him in. Then whoever it was killed her, took her out to that tree and hung her to make it look like suicide. He could have typed the note before leaving. Or, hell, he had hours. He could have come back and done it." I thought about that a minute. "No, that's no good. Her prints were on the typewriter keys."

She turned to watch me gloomily. "How do you explain that?"

I thought quickly. "He could have forced her to do it."

"Maybe it was you," Baxter said softly. "Maybe you're Raskolnikov, obsessed with your crime."

I looked at her in amazement and she smiled gently at my alarm. "Well, think about it, Sherlock. If you keep crying murder you may force the law to find a culprit."

I realized that Arly had died the last night I'd spent in Dallas. A night I'd spent alone, drinking in a bar I'd never been in before, watching a game on TV that I cared so little about I hadn't even discussed it with the other patrons. I didn't have an alibi. But there was something else. "I don't have a motive."

"She was pregnant," she said coolly.

34

"It wasn't mine. I hadn't seen her in three months and she was only two months along."

"You were jealous. You were so upset over her being with another man you killed her in rage."

"You don't believe that," I answered, reassured by her calm. "I wouldn't be here if you did."

She laughed. "You're right. But it's not an implausible scenario."

"No, it's not," I conceded. "What about the other? Do you believe it was murder?"

"I don't know," she answered. "All you have is an intuition that she wouldn't kill herself and some ambiguous evidence that suggests she may have been interrupted while planning her evening. Looking at it objectively, it's not really much."

"Well, listen to this," I said, wishing she wouldn't stay so far away. "Will you sit down and listen to what else I found out?"

"Okay," she said, sitting in the farthest chair in the room and putting her feet on the table as a barrier against me. "Shoot."

"Okay," I said, leaning forward with my elbows on my knees, encroaching ever so slightly into the space between us. "Number one, she was pregnant. That could be a motive. Number two, Pickles Offut raped her when she was a teenager, while she was working in the church nursery. It happened more than once. Hell, as far as I know it may still have been going on. She didn't blow the whistle on him because he threatened to bust her boyfriend for growing pot. The day after Arly died, the guy was busted. That's How Toffler. So *he* had a motive. Pickles had a motive. Either one of them could have done it. Then there's Chad Eby. I'm not clear on him. I don't think he knew she was pregnant and he seemed to have accepted her playing around. But there's bad blood between him and Pickles, I'm sure of that."

Baxter tried unsuccessfully to smile. "And I thought I'd found a peaceful country town to write my book in."

I felt sorry for her again. What was I doing, pulling her into this? "Look, Baxter, maybe I should leave you alone. This doesn't really involve you."

"But it does," she answered immediately. "I mean, I'm here, aren't I? Right in the middle of it. And besides," she smiled, ever so slightly, "I took this place because I identified with Arly. At almost anytime in my past, it could have so easily been me. And if it turns out she's been murdered, I can't just abandon her."

7

Bubba's Pizza was a replica saloon out of Matt Dillon's Dodge City. Long bar, early American tables, wagonwheel chandeliers. Oh yeah, red lights. The jukebox was cranking out Stevie Ray Vaughan complaining about the weather over the heads of half the single population of Holler. Or so it seemed to me. Baxter and I stood by the door until I spied a table just being vacated across the room. I lassoed it with my eyes, claimed it as mine, and jumped and hogtied it before anyone else, feeling ridiculously triumphant as we settled into the relative quiet of the corner. She smiled at me and that was reward enough for any man. But not the kind he wants to share.

Chad Eby had materialized out of the crowd and was pulling a chair toward our table. I was surprised to see him and thought he could have waited for an invitation to join us, but as I owed him one it would have been moot. I introduced him to Baxter.

"So you're living at Arly's?" he sidled, giving her the once over. He looked terrible; his cheeks were sunk in shadows beneath his jutting cheekbones, his smile too calm in a face too knife-like. His eyes were veiled, protected; his posture and gestures, the ambience of his presence, cocky and smug. I could tell Baxter didn't like him. She threw her head back like a nervous colt but managed a smile and a nod. I watched her slide across the bench to lean against the wall, increasing her distance from Eby, who noticed it too.

He was sensitive enough that it took some of the puff out of him and that helped things considerably. He turned to me as if to a friend. "Surprised I didn't see you at Mrs. Walbridge's today."

"Why's that?" I asked, trying to encourage him.

"So many people asked her for something to remember Arly by that she let the word out to come over this afternoon and pick out what they wanted. I expected you there taking notes."

I winced at missing the parade of potential suspects, and also at the sudden edge in Eby's voice. The guy changed moods like most people blink. "I wasn't invited," I said easily. "Who else was there?"

He grinned, a quick slash of teeth across his face and then his mouth closed around a snide smile. He looked at Baxter. "He's good at pumping people, don'cha think?"

She laughed nervously. "At least he's upfront about it. He never lets you forget you're talking to the press."

"Even in bed?" Eby asked, dropping his voice a register.

Baxter's eyes flared at the impertinence. "I wouldn't know," she said haughtily. But she'd played into his hand, she'd told him we weren't sleeping together and named herself fair game. He shifted his chair closer to her side of the table, something she had also allowed by giving him space.

To compensate for moving in on her, Chad leaned across the table to me and whispered a conciliatory piece of information. "Sue Toffler was out there and that's strange. She hated Arly."

"Why?" I asked.

Chad leaned back and relaxed momentarily. "Her husband had an affair with Arly."

"When?"

He was still in his nonchalant pose and his voice actually

drawled. "They went together in high school, but that's ancient history. After he married Sue, he saw Arly off and on. The last time was about eight months ago. I was seeing Sue at the time. Then Arly and I hit it off and she dumped How and I dumped Sue and we got together. It seemed neat and tidy from our point of view, sending them back to each other, but Sue took it personal. It was all over town how she badmouthed Arly all the time." He sat up, tense again, suddenly moving to the music. It was ZZ Top's "Sharp Dressed Man." "You wanna dance?" he asked Baxter.

She seemed to say yes without thinking and followed him, throwing me an apologetic smile. I watched them thread their way through the tables to the rapidly filling floor. Eby was a good dancer, just a little tight and restrained as befitted someone of his delicate dignity. He watched Baxter as he shuffled and jerked in front of her, but she had no eyes for him. She was lost in the music, moving in sensuous flowing curves, her hair falling back and forth across her face like a strobe light, revealing emotions frozen in action.

I reached for my beer, saw the glass was empty, and began searching for the waitress. The room was a chamber of noise, filled with bobbing heads that rose and fell as people stood or crouched over their chairs, yelling and gesticulating about something that wouldn't be remembered tomorrow. A lot of the heads were blond, a few red, most nondescript brown. There was no kinky black hair in the room, no brown faces. Bubba's Pizza was evidently for Anglos only.

I spotted the waitress and caught her eye. She came toward me, undulating her hips at eye-level through the crowd, leaving a wake of appreciative male faces. She wore high cowboy boots and tight white shorts. Her sleeveless blouse was halfway unbuttoned and when she leaned close to hear my order I saw a fine mist of sweat on the curve of her breasts. I looked up into her heavily made-up face and watched her pupils amid the peacock flourishes of paint. "Do you know Sue Toffler?"

Her eyes darkened with dislike. It was very definite, very pronounced, but it was gone in a second behind a façade of indifference.

"Sure, who doesn't?" she asked, standing up straight.

"Is she here tonight?"

"I haven't seen her since her old man got busted. Say, whaddaya wanna drink? I got other customers."

I ordered another round and looked back at Eby and Baxter. The floor was packed now and they were pretty close together but still separated. Touching or not, they moved together in a raunchy style of grace and I felt the sting of jealousy. I wouldn't like to be beaten out for Baxter, especially by Eby, but I thought I still had enough distance to feel safe. When they came off the dance floor, she sat next to me and suddenly I wasn't so sure.

Her face was flushed to the barest tinge of color and her eyes were sparkling with energy. She sipped her beer and laughed. "I haven't danced in ages. I feel like a kid again."

"That's me," Chad Eby said, sprawled alone across the booth, his arms spread along the back, "the fountain of youth." Humiliation became him, or maybe he showed his best colors when rising to a challenge. Unabashed, he was charming, generous. "So do you want to know who else came to Mrs. Walbridge's house today?"

Before I could answer, Baxter said, "I want to know what Sue wanted of Arly's."

Chad gave me a "gotcha" grin and leaned forward. "Whatever it was, she didn't find it."

"You mean she left empty-handed?" I asked.

He shook his head. "She took a piece of driftwood, gave some speech about it reminding her of how Arly loved nature. But she looked a long time, and it seemed to me she was looking for something in particular. And then she just stopped, turned around and picked up the driftwood, gave her little spiel and left."

"Did you ask her if she was looking for something specific?" Baxter asked. "You know, offer to help or anything?"

He shook his head. "I don't talk to Sue."

I interjected, "Do you think she could have killed Arly?"

Eby's face fell and he sat back again and looked at me from hooded eyes. "I'm not going to answer that," he said flatly, "because I don't know. You're asking me to put the finger on someone. Hell, I hadn't even heard it called murder until you came along. You invent the question and then pin me for the answer."

"I'm not asking you to finger anyone," I replied, trying to sound calm. "I asked if you thought she could, not if you thought she did. I mean, think about it, there's some logistics involved. I've never seen Sue Toffler but I suspect it would take some strength to hang someone, especially if they were already dead. Strength and a whole lot of cold-blooded guts."

"Nah, she's skinny, not nearly as strong as Arly. And she's flighty, she's an emotional yo-yo. I could see her shooting someone in anger but not anything that takes five minutes of continuity."

"Who could have?"

"Man, you never let up, do you?" Chad swallowed several gulps of beer.

I held him with my eyes, pushing. "I need information. You know this town. Unless of course you're getting nervous and would rather I drop the whole thing."

"I told you how I felt about that in the club. If you're right and this thing has been covered up, you're walking on mighty private territory. You're messing with Pickles Offut and the Department of Public Safety, which is the newfangled name for the Texas Rangers. Pickles' daddy was a ranger and his grand-daddy too. He's the law around here and what he says is the way it is."

I hesitated just a second, then let it out. "Did you know he raped her?"

Eby's face snapped shut so fast it was like a mask had descended. His eyes were dark, lowered. "Yeah, I know that," he muttered. "And I know why she didn't say anything."

"Do you think maybe she was going to say something and he shut her up?"

Eby was angry. "Nah. Not Pickles. With Arly's reputation no one would believe her anyway. If it's anybody, it's How Toffler. He says Arly blew their deal with Pickles and that's how come he got busted." He stopped and his face blanched. "Yeah, well, I'll be going now," he said coldly, standing up. "But I gotta say, man, I think you're really disgusting."

I watched him stalk away, then looked at Baxter. "Let's pick up our pizza and take it back to your place."

She considered the consequences and then nodded. "You're in luck. I think I can handle really disgusting tonight."

8

The outside temperature had dropped to below ninety and it was merely hot. The wind whipping through the car felt almost arid and I found myself enjoying life for the first time in a long while, long enough to make it noticeable. I reached across and took Baxter's hand. She clasped my hand warmly but didn't look at me, instead leaned back into the bucket seat and gazed at the countryside. A nearly full moon lit the rolling hills enough to show the white spotted cattle grazing in the dark. It looked like a benign farmland scene and yet I knew that rattlers and scorpions lurked silently, waiting to strike.

That's how it must have been with Arly's killer. The thought broke my peace. Someone who was around all the time, silently waiting for his moment. Not someone who had had a moment and stalled or avoided it, not someone pushed over the brink by sudden circumstances, but someone who had waited obscurely and then plunged out of nowhere. Someone friendly but basically unstable. Maybe Chad Eby, driven out of control by the knowledge of her pregnancy. But that seemed so soap opera. People didn't do that over pregnancy anymore.

I looked at Baxter. She was watching me and only then did I realize I'd taken my hand back and was gripping the wheel. I gave her a grimace of a smile. "I was thinking about Arly."

She nodded. "It was nice to have those few moments when you forgot about it."

I laughed at myself. "I liked them too. But I keep stumbling over something when I think about Arly. I have to find out what it is that's tripping me up, not letting me think it out smoothly." I downshifted and turned onto the dirt road by the water tower. "You could help me, Baxter," I said, watching her as we drove slowly over the potholes. "I need someone to talk it out with, someone objective who can stand back and look at it. You're new to this town, you have no allegiances or prejudices. Back home there was this old man named Eliot who used to listen to me a lot. Haven't really had anyone since."

We were coming up on the woods and she looked at me and I saw her face for just an instant, saw the apprehension in her dark eyes, and then the shadow fell across us and she was lost from view. "Is that what Arly did for you?" her voice came disembodied, "listen to you?"

I slowed down for an armadillo trundling across the road. It looked at us in the glare of headlights, its eyes pinpricks of red, defying us to challenge its armor. I stopped the car and let it take its time, pulling Baxter across to me and kissing her. She was compliant but noncommittal. Her coolness puzzled me and I let her slide back to her side of the car. "Arly and I were on vacation together," I said, letting out the clutch and easing the car forward. "We never dealt with daily life together, never discussed anything more concrete than whether to go out or call room service." I had deliberately alluded to our times in hotel beds to hurt Baxter, to get back at her for disappointing me with her coolness. But she seemed to like my answer.

"So your relationship was more intuitive than analytical," she said without rancor.

We'd come to the corner store and the streetlamp illuminated the interior of the car enough for me to see her. She was smiling and looked so damn pretty I forgave her quixotic twists. Besides, an analytical mind was just what I needed at the moment. That it came encased in an attractive female body didn't bother me a bit. As I turned onto the road I saw Hauper's Trans Am parked in the shadow and just a glimpse of a figure in the phone booth. "Have you met your neighbors?" I asked.

Baxter laughed. "Chad was right. You never do let up. No, I have not met my neighbors. But if my stomach doesn't meet some of this pizza, I think I'm going to faint."

I threw the transmission into second and came out of the corner throwing gravel, gunned it and shot down the road beneath the trees. I figured everyone around would think it was the Trans Am, except the guy at the phone booth, and he would know there was another hot-rodder in the neighborhood. Not that I take it seriously, of course. If I was serious I'd trade in this old Celica and modify something with a few less miles on it. Soup it up just a little so it was quiet and then whip it on them when they're least expecting it. I laughed and killed the engine, coasting off the road and into Arly's yard. Baxter's, I reminded myself.

There was really no confusing the two. Arly had been unrestrained high spirits while Baxter was the quiet, serious type. A good analogy would be a high mountain stream tumbling over rocks, exhilarating in its quickness, the sunlight flashing off its facets, compared to a deep river meandering through a valley, filled with shadows from the overhanging trees, moved by a current hidden in its depths. I was curious about the current, and while we sat at the kitchen table eating pizza I dropped a few probing questions to see what came up.

Her father was from a New England banking family and her mother the descendent of Southern planters. They'd met in Washington during the War, had a whirlwind romance, and married in the full regalia of a military wedding beneath the magnolias. They'd tried for ten years to have a child and when Baxter came along they knew they'd never have another so they gave her the boy's name.

"It was just the beginning of my confusion," Baxter said ruefully. "Suffice it to say they weren't actualized people. They didn't like each other but were brought up under strict codes of propriety, so they didn't abuse each other except through me. I got the brunt of their disappointment and it seemed like there was nothing I could do to please them." She let out a big sigh and helped herself to another slice of pizza.

"So I decided, not quite out of thin air, that the fault was mine, and I tried very hard to be good. But I could never figure out what they wanted. Every time I thought I knew, I acted on it and I was always wrong. So then, somewhere in the netherworld of my child's mind, I decided if I did the opposite of what I thought they expected me to, then I would be right. This met with some initial success." She stopped and studied me. "Do you really want to hear all this?"

"Very much," I answered around a mouthful of pizza.

She picked up her fork and toyed with the piece on her plate. "It worked to the extent that it kept them off balance and they left me alone. But when I went away to college, I became confused. I gravitated toward people who didn't like me because unconsciously I knew they were right, my whole life was a lie, and I needed them to affirm the truth of that. I did special projects for professors who I knew were misogynists because I thought I could live up to their expectations and be rewarded, but I'd do excellent work and they hated me for it. I was attracted to men who only wanted sex from me and then I'd try to reform them, or I'd go out with decent guys, drag them into bed and brag of my experience." She cut off the tip of the slice but then laid her fork down and pushed the plate away.

46

"I finally got some insight into what I was doing through a child's game. I was over at this guy's house and his children from a previous marriage were visiting. They'd play this game where they'd ask a question and you were supposed to say the opposite of what you meant. I couldn't do it! They asked if I wanted to go to the park with them and I was supposed to say no, because I really did. But I got lost in the opposites. I knew they wanted me to say no so I'd say yes. It was very embarrassing. This guy kept looking at me like I was incredibly stupid. I went home feeling like two cents. But I was able to shrug it off and I forgot about it. Then my mother got sick. I went home to be with her and through all those months, watching the cancer eat her up from the inside, I struggled to do and say the right things.

"But it was too much for me. I knew I was supposed to love my mother but I didn't feel like I loved her. People would say 'isn't this hard on you?' and I'd tell them it wasn't. Some of them said I should become a nurse because I was so cheerful all the time. But I was in torment. When she died I became hysterical and couldn't stop laughing. My father was torn up about it and really tried to help me. When I realized he loved me, I attempted suicide." Her face was hidden behind her hair. When she raised her eyes to me there were tears glistening on her lashes. "He put me in a very good, very expensive hospital, and I was lucky to have a competent doctor. Eventually, I got well."

"You say that so easily, 'got well.' It must have been a long, hard haul."

"Three years," she said. "Not all as an in-patient. The last two I lived near the clinic and finished college. That was its own hell."

"In what way?"

She shrugged, biting her lip. "After I'd seen all my old patterns and what they'd done to me, I had to give them up. But I didn't have anything to replace them with and I floundered a lot. People weren't kind. I was socially inept and they ridiculed me, picked on me. There's always a bully around looking for someone who can't defend herself. Maybe if I'd told everyone I was fresh from the loony bin they would've been more generous, but I didn't want to do that. I wanted to be well, not someone carrying this label of 'recovering psycho.'"

"Isn't that what you're doing now?" I asked, as gently as I could. "I mean, writing your book and all."

She stopped breathing for an instant, looking at me, and then gulped in air and let it out with a big sigh. "It's for all those people who mistreated me in college. I want them to know what I'd been through and how much they hurt me."

"Revenge?" I asked.

"If that's what the truth is, then yes, revenge."

"The truth doesn't need your book to exist, any more than those people need to read it to know they were mean. What I care about here is what reliving it could do to you. Maybe you should put it all behind you, be well, go on with your life."

"Maybe it's like with you and Arly," she suggested. "She's dead, gone, part of the past. But you won't bury her until you know why. Maybe I'm looking for something in my journals that will tell me why this all happened." She gave me a trembling, tentative smile.

I touched her knee with mine beneath the table, conceding she might be right. But all I could say was, "You look so pretty when you smile," and she rewarded me with another, stronger one. Sloughing off the melancholy mood, I asked, "You want to go for a walk in the moonlight?"

Her voice was soft, barely above a whisper. "Last night I discovered I can watch it going down from my bed. Would you like to see?"

I held my hand out across the table. She met me halfway and then led me down the tunnel hall to the bedroom. I stood in the door while she opened the drapes, reaching high to spread them apart with her arms. Silhouetted against the huge silver moon, she was a willowy line of limber shadow. I glanced around quickly to catch my bearings and saw the longhorns still hanging over the bed. I was glad she'd kept them; they seemed an emblem of Arly's strength, her bouyant good humor.

I turned around to look at Baxter. She stood her distance, waiting for me to lead her. "Come here," I said, and when she stood before me, I kissed her and felt her tremble against me. She was so shy and frightened I pulled her under the covers fully clothed and we lay side by side watching the moon slide behind the trees. I could feel her relaxing against me and when I felt her ready I started real slow. By the time the moon left us in darkness, I could feel her heartbeat against the palm of my hand.

9

The next morning I drove over to the county prison farm to visit How Toffler. The air was heavy but not yet saturated with heat, and the drive on farm-to-market roads reminded me of my home town. I felt comfortable, light on my feet and quick of mind. The day was new, I was fresh from bed, and I had a challenging encounter in front of me. Best of all, Baxter waited at my journey's end.

The prison farm loomed ahead, breaking my peaceful reverie. Surrounded by high, chain-link fences topped with two feet of barbed wire, it was a squat cluster of nondescript buildings behind a large sign commanding all visitors to stop. I obliged, of course; I never tackle authority physically. The guard confirmed the wisdom of my attitude. He was young and stupid, his billyclub and pistol butt continual props for his conversation, which wasn't much. He let me in the main gate but there was still another fence, replete with barbed wire, before I was in the yard itself. I parked my car and went into a trailer with OFFICE painted on the side in huge, black letters.

This man was older, thicker, but just as physical in his approach. He stood up when I came in and let me assess the pure bulk of him, then sat back down to the accompaniment of his chair's complaints. He asked my business, eyed me hard for a minute when I said I was a reporter, then he signed the pass and asked me to wait at the picnic tables outside.

There was a yellow fiberglass roof over the tables, metal tables with feet that curved up to hold the bench. Unilinear, efficient, and cheerless. I sat in the only slightly cooler shade and wished a breeze would waft my way.

I had never imagined a prison camp so quiet. I could hear the flies buzzing, the telephone ring inside the trailer. From far off a meadowlark sang occasionally and I began listening for it, trying to guess if it was moving, when the trailer's air conditioner kicked on and drowned the bird out.

The buildings housing the prisoners were silent in the heat rays bouncing off the macadam surrounding them. The tops of the buildings were open except for bars, creating airways. I could make out the shadowy motion of a ceiling fan in the one closest to me. No wonder there was no activity, the suckers didn't enjoy the comforts of air-conditioning. I heard a door close and saw two men come out and walk toward the gate. One was a guard; the other, I guessed, was Howard Toffler.

He was a big man, solid as a prize bull. The short sleeves of his prison shirt were rolled up and the muscles in his arms glistened with sweat in the sun. He had thick curly black hair and heavy eyebrows. His face was round, his cheeks full and burnished almost copper colored. His neck was huge, his stride mammoth. The guard had to trot beside him.

The guard stayed by the gate and Toffler came toward me with wary eagerness. I introduced myself as a reporter for the Dallas *Spur*. His small dark eyes watched me carefully and I knew I wasn't dealing with someone as dumb as Kerrie Hauper or as easily manipulated as Chad Eby. I offered to buy him a soft drink from the machines behind us but he refused and we sat down across from each other. The guard

51

was a good distance away but our mutual desire for privacy caused us to lean on our arms on the table, close but keeping a carefully defined distance between us.

I began slowly. "I'm doing an investigation of Texas law enforcement. I'd like to ask you a few questions."

"I got lots of time," Toffler drawled, without emotion. "How many answers I got depends on the questions."

"What do you know about Pickles Offut?"

His eyes closed up until they were narrow cracks with headlights shining out. "About as much as anyone else around here."

"Do you think he's a good law officer?"

Toffler laughed, a short, quick bark. "You're asking the wrong man. He just busted me and threw away the key."

"Don't they have due process down here?"

"Yeah, sure. I can't post bail. Pickles made sure of that. So I sit and rot until the judge makes room for my case on his calendar."

"What do you think will happen when you go to trial?"

"I'll get out on probation. Probably a fat fine. Have to break my balls paying it back for a few years and be stuck under Pickles' thumb until probation is up. This stretch here is just another little turn of the screw. Just to make sure I get the message."

"Do you?"

He snorted in disgust. "Shit yeah, man. The message is: Get out from under Pickles."

"But you *were* growing pot. I've heard it from several people."

"So what? I've been growing pot for ten years. Why does he bust me all of a sudden? It's his whim, man. Nobody can live under whimsical law."

"So get rid of Pickles."

He grinned, his cheeks puffing into Santa Claus balls.

"Ain't nobody told you the story about Pickles' daddy and grand-daddy?"

"I've heard it."

"Shit, man, no wonder you're not getting anywhere. You're a Yankee, you won't never understand what goes on in Texas."

I ignored that. "Word is you thought Arly Walbridge was responsible for getting you busted."

He lost his humor. "Yeah? Out of whose mouth?"

I took a calculated risk. "Chad Eby."

"Hell! There's a flake for you."

"Is that your answer?"

"Maybe I got no answers," he glowered.

"Did you know Offut raped Arly in Sunday school?"

He leaned away and squinted at me, a camouflaging gesture. "So what?"

I stifled my outrage, worked at keeping my voice even. "You see no offense in that?"

"Wasn't entirely his fault. Arly was sexy and she knew it, even at sixteen."

"So you don't blame Offut at all?"

Toffler shrugged. "I ain't saying it was right, but it'd been going on for years. If she was going to yell rape she should've done it before she come of age."

"Was it still going on?"

He grinned that I didn't know, and I knew he wasn't going to tell me. "I didn't keep up with Arly's love life."

"Love," I hissed. "That's got nothing to do with love. Anyway, you were the one she was supposedly protecting. I don't hear any gratitude."

The chuckle came from deep in his throat. "Sure, I accidentally benefited from an arrangement between Pickles and Arly. But I was something she had of value. When she was ready to quit playing, she didn't consider me."

"Is that what you think then? That Arly told Offut she'd blow the whistle on him, that she'd bust him even if it meant he busted you?"

He leaned so close I could smell his breath. "I know this for a fact. She visited Pickles at his home the night before she died. And she come away real upset."

"Over what?"

"Ask Pickles."

I hit him with the question while he was still close to me. "Did you know she was pregnant?"

His head jerked and then he squinted and leaned back a fraction of an inch. "Who told you that?"

"It was in the coroner's report."

"Whose was it?"

"Any ideas?"

"Eby's probably. But with Arly, who knows? She was always disappearing for days at a time. Just up and went and never said nothing other than that she'd been to Austin or Corpus or South Padre. I'm sure she didn't go those places alone. She wasn't the hermit type."

"Was she the type to commit suicide?"

His mouth closed hard. "What else would it be?"

"Murder."

He slapped the table hard and let out a high-pitched yell. "Excuse me," he said, laughing at my reaction. "I'm half Comanche. The other half's German. I love a good fight."

"You think there's going to be a fight?"

"I think there's going to be a bloody massacre."

The guard was approaching. As if he had eyes in the back of his head, Toffler stood up. "Time's up. Gotta go."

"Time's up. Gotta go," the guard said.

I stood up too. "I'd like to come back and talk some more," I suggested.

Toffler grinned. "If you live that long."

54

10

As I drove away from the prison camp, I thought about Toffler being half Comanche and half German, and how he looked like a brown version of Thor. His battle yell had been pure animal, triumphant with joy, and I thought he'd probably been a good match for Arly in bed. I could see they would be drawn to each other, regardless of his wife, and I could also see why she would tire of him, his intensity, the demanding fire of his ego. The guy radiated challenge.

I didn't believe he'd known she was pregnant. There was too much surprise in the jerk of his head. I felt the same way about Eby. When I'd told him, he kind of collapsed momentarily. I could see myself doing the same if I was told I'd fathered a child. It's not reassuring news. So if I stuck to this soap opera motive of unwanted pregnancy, I could eliminate Eby and Toffler as suspects. But not Offut. She had visited him and they had quarreled. The next night she was murdered. That was suspicious, or would have been if anyone was investigating. But no one was because they'd named it suicide.

There was something I was missing here, some key connection. It didn't add up. I knew it was because I was approaching everything through this soap opera angle of the unwanted pregnancy, and was actually relieved to see it wasn't working out. But that left me nowhere.

There was the deal with Pickles. Eby and Toffler knew about it, were so familiar with it it hardly ruffled a feather. An act that made me grind my teeth, they shrugged off. The innuendos were that she'd continued sleeping with him for some years, maybe even until she'd died. So maybe it was Offut's child, maybe he couldn't afford a scandal and did it. But Eby had said nobody would believe Arly if she did blow the whistle. If her reputation was too soiled to support a rape charge it wouldn't support a paternity suit. Anyway, with Offut's proclivities, he must have had practice dealing with sudden mothers. Surely he had figured out something better than killing them.

Which left me, again, with nothing. I'd turned west out of the camp, taking winding back roads randomly, edging toward Austin. I hadn't been thinking about my driving and that's why it struck me odd that the same truck should be behind me. It was one of those high, toy trucks kids drive, big tires and tinted windows, following steadily about fifty feet behind. I saw a sign for a viewpoint and took the turn without warning. I shot up the hill, expecting to see the truck sail past in my rear view mirror. But it followed me.

Then I realized I'd trapped myself. If How hadn't made that remark about my longevity, I probably would have stopped and walked back to reconnoiter. It wouldn't have been the first time someone sought me out to give information on the sly. But the combination of the warning and the tinted windows shot me straight into cops and robbers and I reminded myself it was a murder I was poking around. I stepped on the gas and left the truck in a cloud of dust and gravel.

The road wound around the edge of a small mountain, or a big hill, depending on what you compare it to. It was pretty high for a Midwestern boy like me, and the steep slope to the valley below was studded with cactus and other prickly inhabitants. Then again, it couldn't have been that high because I was at the top in less than a minute. There were enough turns on the road that I couldn't see him. I shut off my engine and sat there in a settling swirl of Texas sand, waiting for him. After a minute I realized I couldn't hear him either.

I grinned and then laughed out loud. The sucker was probably lost, following me because he figured I was going somewhere. When he saw me come up here, he turned around at the bottom and went back the way he came. The simplest explanation is usually the truth, Eliot used to say. I was letting my imagination run away with me, just because Toffler had put that suggestion in my mind. I was usually stronger than that. I was the one who manipulated people, I played them like an organ, with all the stops and pedals tuned in unison until they broke forth in the song I wanted to hear. But I couldn't do that if I let someone play with my pipes.

I was a little worried as I started my car and eased back down the hill. Not about my pursuer, I'd forgotten him, but about my state of mind. If I couldn't keep cool through this, I may as well shuck the whole thing right now. I was over my head, AWOL from work, and the only sheep crying wolf. Maybe Arly's death had hit me even harder than I thought and I was just stumbling around catching at straws that would disprove some part of it.

The pickup was parked alongside the cliff up ahead. Slowing down, I watched it but couldn't see past the windows, so I pulled up in front and twisted around to look back at it. Nothing moved. I shut off my engine and listened. Only the sound of a locust somewhere on the hill. Opening my door, I got out, watching the cab. Nothing. I scanned the immediate area, the scrubby brush, the trail going down. A lizard watched me.

Gingerly I approached the cab, calling out, "Hello there." No answer. My scalp prickled with sweat. I leaned close and knocked, then opened the door. No one. The cab was as clean as a rental car.

There was only the trail. I crossed the road and looked down the steep twisting path that disappeared in thickets below. I started down, trying to find fresh footprints, even crouched to study the trail closer, and then I got a sensation of how absurd I was, acting like an Indian scout just because I was in Texas.

The land fell away below me, green, cultivated, slashed by creeks and rumpled by hills, the last arable land before the arid West began. This place where Arly lived was on the edge of Southern civilization; behind me stretched the plantation lands of the bayou, Natchez and Biloxi, Montgomery and Savannah. She was a descendent of the melancholy history of the Confederacy and no matter how little import we Yankees put on that, to a Southerner it's a big deal. Arly lived just north of the Balcones Escarpment, where high-tech comes face-to-face with magnolias. I met her in the other world and she was dynamite. She was vivacious and charming and strong and resilient. She could have made it easily over there. But she'd stayed here, mired in the past, claimed in the end. I wondered why she had stayed, if it was out of loyalty to a way of life she hadn't chosen but would honor. No, that couldn't have been it—she'd raised hell all over town. More likely, it was a place she knew, where she could choose her battles. I heard the truck start above me and knew I couldn't say the same.

Even running I didn't get there in time to get his license number. All I got was a cloud of chalky dust floating lazily to earth and the distant squeal of tires as he hit the paved road. I didn't even bother to try my key. I walked straight to my hood and saw what I knew. He'd taken the distributor cap. I couldn't believe how stupid I'd been.

After I'd been walking for what felt like hours, an old geezer picked me up in his rattletrap truck. When I told him about some kids stealing my distributor at the lookout, I had no trouble building up an appropriate degree of anger. I was still kicking myself. The old guy tch-tched over my trouble and said something generally derogatory about kids.

"Maybe you know these guys," I said, describing the truck.

"Cain't say as I do," the craggy face answered. "See a lot of trucks like that 'un but cain't say about one in perticular. Most of 'em is city boys, my guess."

He dropped me at a grocery-gas store and I phoned Triple-A to come get me. I told the guy the model cap I needed and he said he'd pick one up on the way out. He seemed to know exactly where I was, which bothered me because I had no idea. I couldn't let my paranoia extend to Triple-A. They were white knights of the highway. Well, maybe not that good, but there's a difference between assessing danger and seeing it everywhere. I had to get hold of myself, start seeing things rationally again. If only I could find some thread of evidence, some link that promised to lead somewhere, I could hang on. But if I continued to feel like a fish out of water it was time to get some distance.

No, that would be running, I told myself, going into the store succinctly named Convenience. It wasn't some kid who stole my distributor cap, it was the murderer. Or someone acting in his interest. Maybe there was more than one.

A tired, old lady stood watching me from behind the counter. I explained I was waiting for the tow truck and bought a pack of gum. "Ever see a tan and bronze high wheel pickup around here? With tinted windows?"

"Who's it belong to?" she asked impatiently.

"That's what I'd like to know."

"They do somethin' to you?"

She wasn't generous with her answers. I eased up a little.

"I'm interested in buying the truck. Been looking for one like that for a long time."

She lost interest. "A truck's a truck. What's the difference?"

"This one's special." I played it out. "It's got tinted windows so you can kiss your girl in the drive-in."

"That's not all you do behind them winders, I'll warrant. Now you just go on out of here. Wait for your tow truck man outside."

I was glad to oblige. Her company was pleasant to be rid of. I waited in the shade, leaning against the building chewing my Juicy Fruit. I even put my foot up on the wall behind me and wished for a Stetson to pull down over my eyes. If I *was* the Lone Ranger, the killers would come to me. They'd be so sure I'd find them out they'd try to off me first. Well, I wasn't, and if whoever had stolen my distributor cap had been the killers they'd been as stupid as me. It was such a puny gesture: stealing your horse and making you walk back to town was kid stuff, tactics learned from Grade B westerns. And they didn't even work then—the hero always found another horse. Mine was Triple-A.

The killers should have offed me on the spot or left me alone. Another five minutes and I would have given up. Now I knew someone was trying to discourage my nosing around. Or then again, hell, maybe it *was* some kids on a prank. Maybe I was seeing shadows of windmills.

The Triple-A man was named Gus and he kept up a steady put-down of today's youth from the moment I got in his truck. I asked him about the pickup and drew a blank, except it was probably some "frat twerp from the university." Gus was a nice guy but I soon gave up on getting any information out of him. I did learn one thing while we were replacing the distributor cap. He'd voted for Pickles and would do it again. I thanked him and let his dust settle good before following him down the hill.

60

I'd wasted an afternoon and was going home empty-handed of any new answers. But the question had just been changed to bold type. I decided to visit Sue Toffler. Anyone who hated Arly as much as Eby said she did should be willing to talk dirt about her. And then I'd swing by Mrs. Walbridge's and see how much of a chip off the old block Arly had been. I was hoping she'd gotten her spunk from her mother.

11

I knew the Toffler place was on Holler Creek Road. As I drove along the shady bank of the creek I thought of the story Arly had told me about how Holler got its name. It was originally called Hollering Woman Creek because back in the 1800s a white woman was kidnapped by the Comanches and taken down to the brook and tortured to death. They say at certain times you can still hear her screaming. Whether that part is true or not, the town found the memory too grisly and shortened the name to Holler in the 1950s.

That made me think about Toffler being half-Comanche and how Arly was hung by the river. Maybe it was an Indian habit to take your victims to water so you could wash their blood off afterwards. He'd seemed awfully pleased when I called it murder, like a warrior who had found an opponent. Or maybe he just liked a good fight. I had a hunch he knew who did it but I didn't think he'd done it himself. It hadn't gained him anything because he was in jail. And I didn't think he'd sent the frat twerp after me from behind bars.

His spread was a pretty stone ranch house behind a curved drive. A barn was off in the distance, beyond a couple of empty corrals. In the field behind the barn half a dozen horses grazed, too far away to be disturbed by my arrival. There was a Ranchero in the carport and an empty space beside it. The house was so quiet I suspected Sue wasn't home. I walked around to the back and saw their vegetable garden, a grackle sitting on their scarecrow. Just to make sure I went to the back door and knocked, but I was certain no one was home.

I hadn't been in a barn since I was a kid and theirs was so picturesque, ruddy red with white crossboards, I thought I'd go over and take a look. I was kind of surprised to find a padlock and chain on the front. The windows were covered with straw piled up in what looked like flat boxes built as decoy shutters. I walked around to the back of the barn and came face-to-face with a black brahman bull in the pen around the back door, which was open but questionably usable.

The bull looked bored. His lids drowsed heavily on his eyes and his mouth worked lethargically at his cud. Even his tail only lifted dispiritedly to flick at flies. I climbed up onto the fence.

His eyes followed me, the lids lifting unintelligently over the dark bulbous pupils, the unflickering herd instinct following movement. He gave a lazy slap of his tail and yawned. Then he dropped his knees and groaned himself onto the ground for a nap. I was elated. It was the perfect time for bulls to take siesta. I slid down the fence and into the pen, slipped nimbly into his stall and through a wooden gate into the barn.

Hanging from the rafters by ropes, creating an upside-down forest in the cavern of the barn, were drying marijuana plants. I took in the sweet smell of curing hemp, dumbfounded. I couldn't imagine Pickles busting the field and neglecting to search the barn. That could only mean he was in on the business and the bust was phony. So Arly had bargained for nothing, because Pickles would never bust himself. Yet he had done exactly that. It could only have been to cover something up. Something serious, like murder.

I heard a dog bark and then a car door slam. Scurrying back through the stall door, I edged into the sunlight of the pen and saw what I was afraid of. The bull was standing guard now, his eyes wide open and his tail twitching nervously. I slid along the wall a good five feet before he saw me. He was confused between me and the approaching barking dog and I took advantage of it and jumped onto the fence just as he lowered his head. I dropped to my feet on the other side and backed away in genuine alarm when the bull butted not so playfully against the boards between us. A tall brunette walked toward me and I managed a sickly smile.

"That's some bull you got there," I said.

"What are you doing here?" she demanded. She was as skinny as Eby had said, the kind of girl we called Olive Oyl in high school. But her figure had become fashionable and she was all decked out in the latest pleated pants and tight jersey shirt without a bra. Her breasts were like pancakes with a dollop of butter in the middle. And she had big feet. I hate women with big feet.

"I came to visit," I said pleasantly. "No one answered my knock up at the house and I thought you might be down here by the barn. So I came to look and your bull there, he charged me soon as I turned the corner."

The Doberman was still barking but a safe five feet away. I figured I could jump for the fence if he attacked. "Shut up, Wolf," she told him meanly, raising her hand as if to hit him. It was enough. He curled into a ball at her feet and watched me carefully. "Who was it you wanted to visit?" she asked, not giving an inch.

"You," I said. "You are Sue Toffler, aren't you?"

"What if I am? Who are you?" She had a narrow thin face pinched by dislike of me.

"Name's Frank James. I just came from visiting your husband."

"So?"

"I wanted to talk to you too, if I could."

"What about?"

"Arly Walbridge."

She sneered. "That trash? I got nothing to say about her."

"Do you know she's dead?"

"Sure I know. It's nothing to me. Good riddance, she did us all a favor."

"So you believe it, about it being suicide?"

Her mouth closed and her eyes flashed open wide. "You a cop or something?"

I shook my head. "Reporter."

"What're you doing?"

"Investigating Arly's murder."

Her eyes flared again at the word. "Come on up to the house," she said, turning her back and walking away, hiding her face by keeping ahead. I figured it was as much to keep me away from the barn as from any desire to get me into the house, but as soon as we walked into the refrigerated living room she peeled her shirt off and confronted me from across the wet bar. "We're nudists, How and me. Hope you don't mind."

I shrugged, lost for words. Her breasts looked a lot better uncovered. There was a little droop to them that gave them some substance and I wondered how one of them would feel in my hand. Cold, I told myself, trying not to watch them as she brought me a beer. I took the bottle and turned to look out the picture window facing the pool. "Nice place you got here," I said lamely.

"We were talking about murder," she said. "Who do you think did it?"

I turned to face her—her face, that is. "If I knew that would I be here?"

"Obviously not," she countered quickly, but broke our gaze and walked away. "I was with a friend that night, from six 'til two in the morning."

"I hadn't asked you for an alibi."

"That's what you came here for, isn't it? Everyone knows I hated Arly."

"Does everyone know why?"

"If they didn't I wouldn't have hated her so much."

"Did you kill her?"

"No."

"What were you looking for in the stuff at her mother's?"

She took a deep breath and her breasts flared into my view again. Her nipples were hard in the air-conditioned chill. "Just something," she answered.

"To remember her by?"

"No, obviously not." She turned on her heel and walked back to the bar where she refreshed her drink from a bottle of spritzer. "I'd left some shoes at her house. I wanted them back, that's all. They were brand new." She seemed impressed with the reasonableness of her explanation.

"Did you leave them there while on a social call?"

She laughed, her nostrils flattening, her eyes squeezing shut. "More or less," she finally answered. "I paid a call on her."

"And left without your shoes?"

"Yes," she said, smirking. "Because I threw them at her. I was so mad I threw them straight at her, hit her with one of them too. Then I tore out of there and seethed all the way home. It was hours before I realized I'd lost my shoes. That was Arly, for you. Always getting the last laugh." She wasn't amused anymore; she looked close to crying. "It's no crime, is it," she whined, "to want my shoes back?"

"When did all this happen?"

"That afternoon. The afternoon of the night she died."

"What were you mad at her about?"

"The same old thing. I saw her with How again. And I just couldn't take it anymore. She dances in and out, picking him up when she wants him and dropping him back in my lap when she doesn't. And he always goes. Just like a dumb yo-yo. I gave her hell, that's what I did. I called her trash and a few other things I won't repeat in mixed company. I threw my shoes at her and stormed out of there."

"Why didn't you just go ask Mrs. Walbridge about the shoes?"

She was sassy again. "You know the answer. What kind of game are you playing?"

"Tell me the answer."

"It wouldn't have looked real good that I went storming over there and then she was murdered," she answered sarcastically.

"How'd you know it was murder?"

She hooted. "Nobody believed Arly killed herself. She was too mean."

"Why don't you all protest? Find out the truth?"

"Yeah, well, with Arly, who cares, you know?"

12

Compared to Sue Toffler, Baxter was touched with divinity. Her body was rounded and soft in the right places, her hands massaging my shoulders and neck were gentle, her scent some tweedy perfume that reminded me of ripe corn fields beneath a harvest moon. I could even smell her breath coming over my shoulder and it carried some ineluctable quality that inspired me to turn and catch her mouth with my own. Her fingers stopped momentarily, then resumed.

"Chad came over this afternoon," she purred.

So he was Chad to her now. "What was he driving?"

"I beg your pardon?"

"What kind of car did he drive?" I repeated, shrugging her hands away and moving to the refrigerator for a beer.

"It was a truck," she said, baffled. "A pickup with a camper on back."

"Was it tan and bronze and set up high on its wheels with tinted windows?" I took a big draught of beer.

"No. It was white, old enough so the fenders and hood were rounded, and it had a blue and yellow camper on the back, with a boat on top. A canoe, actually," she laughed, warming to detective work. "I even remember the license, because we talked about it. ZZZTOP. He wanted just two Zs but someone already had that one. It's the name of a band."

"I know," I said, disappointed. Sipping my beer, I told her of my adventure on lookout hill.

She didn't seem worried. "It's probably a coincidence, don't you think? How Toffler probably just said that, and then some kids pulled a prank. I mean, you don't threaten someone's life and then steal their distributor cap. The two acts don't connect."

I started pacing the floor, taking a sip of my beer every few steps. "They weren't threats, they were warnings. Maybe they were trying to be friendly. Or maybe the next time they'll mean business. But if they were trying to discourage me, they should have left me alone. Is that a tactical error or enticement into a trap? God, I wish something jelled in this whole thing. I wish I could find just one piece of unambiguous evidence."

"It would be enough," she said quietly, watching me walk back and forth in front of her, "if you could establish it was murder. Then you could let the authorities take over."

I stopped in front of her, flabbergasted. "The authorities are the ones covering it up."

"There's always someone above them. Go to Austin, talk to the attorney general. You don't have to solve the case yourself."

I'd been given that advice before, along with an admonishment that it was my job to report the news, not create it. I'd ignored it then, too. "Come over to see Mrs. Walbridge with me," I suggested lightly.

Baxter knew the way of course but that wasn't the only reason I wanted her along. I was beginning to understand a little bit about Southern gentility and knew the old woman would trust me more if I came escorted by a lady. Besides, I liked Baxter's company. She was easy and giving; you'd almost be tempted to call her complacent, but when she talked you knew she had a mind and used it. Intelligent, pretty women are hard to find. Add rational to that list and they knight you if you find one. I was beginning to like the sound of Sir before my name.

The only catch was Eby. I hated the surge of jealousy I felt; it foreboded ill of the future. And worst of all, it clouded my perception of Eby so I couldn't see him without an ax to grind. That was dangerous.

"What did Chad have to say?" I asked casually, trying to keep any rancor from his name.

"Oh, he only stayed a minute. He said he was just checking in on our progress. I hadn't seen you all day so there was nothing to tell. We talked a little bit and then he left. He said he was going camping on the Purgatorio and invited us to join him if we wanted to get away from the world. He seemed sincere, drew us a map and everything."

"You sure I was included in the invitation?"

She laughed. "He mentioned you by name. In fact, I had the feeling it was you he wanted to come and I was a pleasant tag-along."

"He picked an odd time to leave," I mused.

"Well, he left you a map where to find him."

"Yeah, but as long as I'm here, he could pull all kinds of shit incognito, everybody expecting him to be canoeing on the Purgatorio."

"You mean, like borrowing someone's truck and stealing someone's distributor cap?"

I shrugged. "He warned me twice verbally to leave it alone. Maybe he's trying to impress upon me that this really could be dangerous."

"Maybe it's true," she murmured from the darkness on her side of the car.

I shook my head. "Not yet. I can sense danger, it prickles the hair on the back of my neck. As long as I don't know anything I'm safe."

"So why are we going to see Arly's mother?"

I smiled noncommittally. "To pay our condolences."

"Yeah, sure," she said. "You could have done that the first day you were in town. Turn left here."

We pulled into a gravel driveway leading to a shadowed lot. The house was a box bungalow with a silent air conditioner protruding from a window. There were lights on inside but the drapes were closed and the porch was dark. I followed Baxter up the few steps and stood behind her while she rang the bell. She didn't ring again, though the old lady took a long time coming. The porch light came on just before the door opened and we were blinded momentarily by yellow buglight. When my vision cleared I saw Arly's mother behind the screen.

There was no mistaking the resemblance. She was a larger, coarser, more worn-down version of Arly. Her face was lined with fatigue but there was Arly's smile making a brave front on her lips. "Oh Baxter," she said, "it's you." With easy grace, she unlatched the door and let us in.

The living room was crowded with heavy furniture and old lady mementos of a long life. There was a picture of Arly on the wall, Arly laughing in the sun, her hair blowing in the wind. It would have been my choice of portraits to keep too. She led us through an arch to the dining area, told us to sit down and went on into the L of the kitchen. "What would you kids like to drink?" she asked, turning the fire on under the coffee with a match.

"Coffee's fine," Baxter and I said in unison, laughing in embarrassment.

Mrs. Walbridge brought the cups and sat down heavily across from us. She smiled at Baxter. "Look at her, in town a week and already has a young man squirin' her around. 'Course she's so pretty I'm not surprised. My Arly was pretty too. Did you know my daughter, Frank?"

Baxter had introduced us by the door, not mentioning my profession. "I was an admirer of Arly's," I said softly.

She nodded and smiled. "She had a lot of those." Her voice rose at the end and I realized her throat was constricted from the effort not to cry.

I have this theory that when sorrow becomes insuppressible the only way out is anger, and if that anger can be channeled correctly, justice can sometimes be done. I said gently, "She had some enemies, too."

Mrs. Walbridge eyed me coolly a moment and then got up for the coffee. Nothing was said while she poured each of us a cup, the aroma filling the room.

Beyond us darkness had settled over Holler. What Mrs. Walbridge said next would determine if I walked away forever or if I penetrated that darkness in the name of justice. She was a worn, frayed old woman who had lost her only child. But she was Arly's mother and I was counting on some fight being left behind those brooding eyes. I got it.

"I know who you are," she said, settling at the table and fixing me with a clear steady gaze. "You're a reporter from Dallas and you've been talkin' to folks about Arly bein' murdered."

"I'm surprised," I admitted, admiring the way she could spit the word out.

"Holly called me. Said she saw you with Chad Eby and then you talked to her alone after he left."

"What was your reaction?" I asked, holding my breath for her answer.

She closed her lips so hard there was a white line around her mouth. When she spoke, her voice barked, short, crisp, "I never believed it."

"You never believed it was suicide?"

Her eyes shot to Baxter with a palpable plea for help.

She came through with exactly the right words. "Frank loved Arly, Mrs. Walbridge. He's trying to make things right."

The old lady stared at her, frozen a moment, and then she visibly relaxed. Her shoulders sagged and her breasts became lost in the folds of her dress. She lifted her hands to the table and folded them together, rumpled veiny hands with long crooked fingers and a simple gold wedding band. She looked right at me through eyes shiny with tears. "I never believed it," she repeated. "My Arly wouldn't do that to herself. You knew her. How full of life she was."

"That's how I felt," I said. "It just didn't sit right. So I've been asking around."

Mrs. Walbridge nodded. "And what did you find out?" She said it cynically, as if she expected nothing.

"A lot of pieces," I said, getting excited, "but no pattern, no piece that fits any of the others. But I think I'm onto something now. And I need your help."

I could see her withdraw a little behind her eyes. "What is it?"

"Two questions. The first is, How Toffler told me Arly visited Pickles Offut the night before it happened. He said they quarreled. Do you know anything about that?"

Mrs. Walbridge nodded. "Yes, she came here afterwards. Said she'd had a fight with Pickles. That she'd hit him and he hit her back. She had a knot on her head where he'd bumped her against the wall."

"What was the fight about?"

"I tried to be a good mother to Arly. She was kind of wild and a lot of mothers wouldn't have listened to some of the things she told me. But with Pickles I drew the line. I knew she'd had a thing with him some years back. And it had all come down on her head when she'd started organizin' and gettin' involved at the mine. She was at his mercy down there, the only prisoner in the county jail. I told her she better be nice to Pickles but she never would. She egged him on like he was the Devil and she wasn't no more afraid of him than any other country bumpkin. But he always bested her. A fool could see he was playin' with her. That she was sincere and tryin' to stand up for what's right in this town was only entertainment to him. He treated her like a cantankerous filly he was goin' to break. When she told me she was intimate with him I wanted to cry out, why you fool! But I didn't. I bit my tongue and I was always here when she'd come around nursin' her bruises. I figured that was the best I could do for her, be in her corner with the bandages and clean water. So when she told me she'd had a fight with Pickles I just shut my mouth up tight and didn't ask nothin'."

"Did you tell the coroner at the inquest?"

She shook her head.

"Didn't you tell anybody about it?" I asked, incredulous.

"I told Pickles," she said.

"What'd he say?"

"He said she was pregnant and must have been crazy with shame. And I said to him, Was it yourn? Just like that, cold to his face. And he said to me a bald lie, 'Mrs. Walbridge,' he says, 'I ain't never touched your daughter.' And I said well then he was callin' her a liar because she'd told me so herself. And then he said it was true but it'd been over a long time."

She stopped and I had to prod her. "Did you ask him about the fight?"

"No. But I told him this, I told him I didn't care what they put on the official report, but I wanted to know what happened to my little girl." She drew in a sharp breath and held it, then deflated. "He said I was overwrought and should see a doctor about gettin' some nerve pills. He sent flowers to her funeral and they had this banner across them that said 'Rest in Peace.' All through the services I kept seein' that banner and it was like his last word on the matter. And I guess I decided maybe it *was* best. She's gone, no matter what else."

74

She raised her cup with trembling fingers and slurped some coffee between her white lips. I felt Baxter's hand on my thigh, warning me to let up on the old lady. But I couldn't yet.

"The second question, Mrs. Walbridge," I said softly, "concerns the people who came over here to take something of Arly's to remember her by."

She raised bleary eyes and nodded at me.

"Who came that day? And what did they take?"

She set the cup down, rattling it against the saucer noisily. "Let me see. Holly came. She wanted a pair of earrin's she'd always admired. Chad took a photograph of him and Arly. Maggie came by and wanted a picture, a sand-paintin' Arly brought back from Arizona one time. Sue Toffler spent a long time pickin' over things. You'd a thought she was at a garage sale. Then she picked up this piece of driftwood I'd seen her kick out of the way a minute before and said she wanted that. I almost said she couldn't have it but she's such a spiteful girl I gave it to her just to get her to go away." She sipped her coffee again and I noticed her hand was steadier now. "And then that little Kerrie Hauper came by with her baby. Such a tiny thing. I enjoyed visitin' with her. I think she was the only one who really loved Arly, except Chad Eby I guess. He hung around a long time, too. He thought you'd be comin'."

I nodded. "What did Kerrie take?"

"Oh, a book is all. A paperback book." She shrugged.

"Of what?" Baxter asked, interested.

"Feminist poetry, I think," Mrs. Walbridge said. "Kerrie was the latest in a long line of people Arly tried to help. She'd told me how she was tryin' to 'raise her consciousness.'" She chuckled. "She was always talkin' like that, tryin' to get people to see what they were doin' to themselves and that they had a choice. Fell on deaf ears mostly, though she would've been proud to see Kerrie choose that book."

"I've met Kerrie," I said. "She could use a little back-bone."

"That Rod Hauper beats her," Mrs. Walbridge bristled. "How much spine would you have livin' under the thumb of someone mean and twice your size?"

I smiled. "I can see where Arly got her fight."

She smiled too and I figured things were about as family as they were going to get. I kept my voice low, almost in a drone, so they had to lean forward to hear me. "I visited Sue Toffler today. She told me something that got me started on a hunch. Would you do one more thing for me?"

"If I can," she answered smoothly.

There was no soft way to phrase it. "Do you have the clothes Arly was wearing when they found her?"

She took a deep breath. "Yes."

"May I see them?"

She looked at Baxter and then back at me, then word-lessly got up and went into another room. We could hear her opening doors in the distance.

"What are you doing?" Baxter whispered.

I shook my head. "Just a hunch."

"Well, you better be right. This is pretty traumatic for her."

"I know that. Sometimes life hurts."

Baxter gave me an apprehensive look but I was saved from her reply by the re-entrance of Mrs. Walbridge. She carried a box wrapped in brown mailing paper. When she set it on the table I saw it had been sent to her from the Department of Public Safety, Office of Sheriff Pickles Offut.

"I never opened it," she said. "Didn't even want to pick it up so they mailed it to me. You go ahead and look, I'll be out on the porch for a spell."

We watched her leave, listened to the creak of the swing. She'd left the door open so she could hear us; she just didn't want to see anything. I tore the box open as quietly as I could. Baxter was at my elbow, watching the process warily. When I had the box unwrapped I hesitated and then lifted the concealing flaps.

Right on top was the silver Navajo bracelet she always used to wear and suddenly I couldn't take it. I went and stood by the door, my shadow falling across the porch next to the creak of the swing, and said, "You do it, Baxter. You didn't know her."

There was a rustling sound and then she said, "Clothes, that's all."

"What kind of clothes?" I heard the bracelet being set on the table and gritted my teeth.

"Bra, panties, blouse, jeans, shoes."

"What kind of shoes?" I asked, my heart quickening.

"Red, sort of like ballet slippers but with a street sole."

"What size are they?"

She was quick because they were almost new. "Nine," she said.

"What size did Arly wear, Mrs. Walbridge?" I asked, listening to the last creak of the swing whine into nothingness.

"Six and a half," she croaked.

There was absolute silence. I spun around to look at Baxter. "That's it," I said, "that's what I needed."

13

I took the box with me, intending to drop by Pickles' office with it in the morning. I left the bracelet on the kitchen table. Baxter was quiet driving home, which was okay by me. I was busy sorting out the new bits and scraps of information.

Except for the box, Mrs. Walbridge really hadn't contributed much. She had confirmed that Arly and Pickles had a fight but didn't know what about. As for the list of suspects picking clues from Arly's stuff, it sounded more like an opportunistic grab bag to me. Earrings she'd always admired. A sandpainting, no doubt worth a lot more than sentiment. The comedy of Sue I'd heard before. And then Kerrie Hauper with her poetry. I looked across at Baxter. "Have you met your neighbors yet?"

"You asked me that already. No."

"That was last night. Slow, aren't you?"

She shrugged. "I didn't come here to socialize."

"You get any writing done today?"

"No. With errands, and Chad's visit, and thinking about Arly, I didn't get settled enough to start. But I will."

"I hope not."

"Why?"

"I don't think it's good for you."

"I don't think it's good for you to be investigating Arly's murder, but I don't see you stopping."

"That's different."

"Why?"

"It's my job."

"Oh. Well, there's all kinds of livelihoods, you know."

"What does that mean?"

"That what we're doing is equally important to each of us."

"But it's different, Baxter." I took the turn by the water tower, then reached across for her hand. "I'm worried about you."

After a minute she said, "I appreciate that. But my villains are all in my head. I don't think you can say the same."

"Maybe that makes mine less dangerous." I pulled into the Haupers' yard and shut off the engine. Baxter's presence in the dark was as palpable as if I held her in my arms, but she was distant, removed, and I didn't like the feeling. "Come on," I said gently, "let's go meet your neighbors." She came along, reluctantly following.

Rod Hauper came to the door. "Yeah?" he asked, peering down from the icy trailer.

"We're your new neighbors," I said in a friendly tone, despite being kicked from behind. "My name's Frank James and this is Baxter McCullough. Thought we'd come and say hello."

"I know who you are," he said. "Come in if you want." He unhooked the latch and walked away.

Kerrie was standing in the kitchen holding the baby. She smiled at us. "Hello," she said brightly. "My name's Kerrie. Did I hear you say Frank and Baxter? Which is which?" She giggled.

I played along with not having met her before. After mindless laughter over getting straight who was who, we stood awkwardly in silence.

Kerrie spoke up. "Why don't you offer them a beer, Rod?"

He was sitting on the couch, looking at us. He hadn't asked us to sit down. "Just ran out," he said. "Was kind of wishin' for one myself."

There was another silence, then Baxter said "Well!" as if it meant something. I held out a minute longer and was rewarded.

"You're the one been pokin' around about Arly," Hauper said.

I nodded. "Did you know her?"

"This ain't no New York City where you don't know your neighbors."

I nodded again, keeping my hands in my pockets. "Did you happen to notice anybody over there the night it happened?"

He grinned. "We went to the picture show. Saw two triple-X movies, didn't we, Kerrie?"

"Yeah, we did," she answered with a quaver in her voice.

"After that," he said slimily, "we was busy. Not payin' any attention to anythin' happenin' outside."

I nodded for the third time, beginning to feel like a plastic dummy. "Well," I said, echoing Baxter. "Just thought we'd stop in and say hello. You're welcome to come visit anytime."

Baxter didn't need to be told to open the door. "Come again," Kerrie called when we were already in darkness outside. The door slammed and we were left with the heat and the crickets.

Baxter jumped right in. "You've got a lot of nerve. Where do you get off telling people we live together?"

"Oh that," I said, unlocking the car and checking to make sure the box was still there. "Forget it. It doesn't matter."

"Not to you, maybe," she said, slamming her door. "It matters a whole hell of a lot to me."

She was still fuming when we got back to her place but not enough to suggest I not come in. She waited until we were safely enclosed in the air-conditioning, all cool and chilled for the night, before beginning again.

"Really, Frank, you must realize how I feel about this."

I tried a ploy that sometimes works. I kissed her before she could open her mouth to say more. She pushed me away.

"How juvenile!" she said, removing herself across the room and turning to stare at me. "Will you at least admit it was cheeky of you to tell them we were living together?"

I shrugged. "Okay, I'm sorry. It was expedient at the time. I didn't want to start right off asking questions."

She relented. "Did you learn anything?"

I shook my head. "Didn't really expect to. Maybe I just wanted to see a wife beater in person."

"Oh. Start a fan club maybe," she said sarcastically.

"I only beat women who want it," I teased.

"That's disgusting."

"Last night you said you liked disgusting."

"Yeah, but not like that."

I came up close and slid my hands up her back beneath her blouse. "How *do* you like it?"

"You know how I like it," she said. And apparently I did.

14

The next morning I took the package of Arly's clothes down to city hall. Teresa Wains was standing at the top of the stairs talking to a woman who looked like a twenties vamp blowing bubble gum. I wondered at this rite of female adolescence that turns wholesome young women into masquerade monsters. My reverie was interrupted by Teresa stilettoing up the hall behind me. "Oh Mr. James," she called, and I was obliged to stop and wait for her.

"I was hopin' you'd come by again," she said breathily, reaching me just as I started off again.

"Why's that?" I asked, shooting a sideways glance and noting her lip gloss was orange today.

"I think you're nice," she giggled, struggling to keep up with me on her heels.

"Great," I said.

"Pickles doesn't though." She looked up at me teasingly.

My interest quickened. "What does Pickles think?"

"He thinks you're in with Chad Eby. You know, *he* never comes around here. I saw him in Bubba's the other night and I asked him why and you know what he said?"

"What'd he say?" I was trying to slow down now but we were already at the door.

"He said he wasn't stupid," she answered, breezing through and flouncing into her perch. She picked up the phone so her fingernails stuck out into the air and punched the intercom with the eraser of a pencil. "Frank James is here." She smiled at me while she listened then she said, "Yes, sir," and hung up. "Have a seat, Mr. James. He'll be right out."

I looked at the uncomfortable bench against the wall and knew it wasn't for me. I walked right over to the door and on through, closing it behind me.

Pickles was angry. "I told you to wait!" he bellowed, half rising from his chair.

I held up the box. "I want to surrender evidence in a murder case."

His mouth snapped shut and he slowly sank back into his chair. "Whose murder?" he asked.

"Arly's. These are the clothes she was wearing."

"So?"

I tossed him the box. "Look at the shoes," I said.

He lowered the box to the desk in front of him, watching me. Then he opened it and fumbled inside and came out with the pair of shiny red shoes. "So?" he asked again, impatient.

"Size nine," I said, watching him look quickly. "Arly wore six and a half."

I waited for his mind to go through the necessary revolutions. He shrugged without conviction. "Doesn't mean anything. So she wore someone else's shoes? She was upset."

"She couldn't have kept them on her feet. If she was coherent enough to pick out that tree and head for it, after typing a note and finding a rope, she was coherent enough to realize she'd be crossing a rocky beach and climbing a steep hill. She'd wear shoes that fit."

He shrugged again. "Maybe. Conjecture, that's all it is."

"Are you serious? This is evidence."

"Of what?"

"Whoever killed her put that shoe in the tree to make it

83

look like suicide, not realizing it wasn't her shoe." I waited for him to agree with me.

"Arly was a tough bugger," he finally said. "Maybe she went barefoot and it was just coincidence that the shoes were there, maybe left earlier by young lovers in a hurry."

"That's a lot of maybe's, Pickles."

"No more than your theory. The shoes are too big. So what?"

"I know whose they are."

"It doesn't matter whose they are. Whoever it is will tell us she left them there earlier. Coincidence, that's all."

"Aren't you at least going to ask?"

Pickles dropped the shoes into the box and leaned back with a big sigh. "No, I'm not," he pronounced. "The case has been officially declared a suicide by the coroner and I see no reason to disallow that decision."

"Not even reasonable doubt?" I pushed.

"If I had reasonable doubt, then I would. But since I don't, I won't. Get it, boy?"

"What would give you doubt?"

"A person with a motive, for starters."

"How about you? You and Arly had a fight the night before she died. You hit her."

He stared at me in hatred.

"And I also know she had plenty of reason to hate you."

His lip curled into a sneer. "She asked for what she got."

"Being murdered? Is that what she asked for?"

"Suicide," Pickles said, "is the official verdict. And I'll believe it until proven otherwise. But if you're asking if I miss Arly, no, I don't. Neither did I kill her. If you're trying to pin me for it, mister, you got a bigger bull by the horns than you might think. I suggest you come up with something a little better than shoes that don't fit."

It was my turn to stare at him in hatred.

"Matter of fact," he drawled, leaning far back in his chair

84

and looking down his nose at me, "I been giving this some thought, believe it or not. And I come to the conclusion that if you *are* right, then one little piece of information that we considered inconsequential may be a clue after all."

I hated him for making me but I bit. "What?"

"She'd had sex shortly before she died."

"Doesn't that suggest something else to your mind, Sheriff?"

"And what would that be?" he asked, his face florid beneath a fixed smile.

"Rape?" I almost shouted. "Raped and murdered maybe?"

His Cheshire cat grin was complete. "But then it could have been any drifter passing through, and by now he might be anywhere. Without evidence there's no cause to open an investigation. Best to let the wounds heal unless we come up with something substantial."

"That's a peculiar outlook for a law officer," I spit out.

"Well, it's my final word, sonny boy. You know, I called your editor this morning and he said he had no idea you were traipsing around down here, disturbing quiet citizens. You're supposed to be in Austin covering the legislature. Why don't you just go on back there and do your job?"

I turned on my heel and walked out in disgust. At the desk I remembered the box and went back to stand in the door. "I want a receipt for that evidence," I said.

He picked up the box and threw it at me. "Get one from Teresa," he said gruffly. "And close the door."

I obliged willingly. She'd already dug the forms out and was putting them in her typewriter. I was amazed to see she could type rather deftly with her lacquered nails. She smiled at me. "Phone number and address?"

I gave her Baxter's. Sitting on the edge of her desk and leaning close I whispered quickly, "What did you mean out there, in with Chad?"

Her breasts fluttered once or twice, threatening to break free from her push-up bra. "About the murder," she whispered, and then louder, "Contents of box, please?"

"What about it?" I asked under my breath, then louder, "Bra, panties, blouse, jeans."

"I don't know. He just said he thought you were in with Chad," she answered softly. Raising her voice, "Is there a value you'd like to place on these, Mr. James?"

I stood up. "One more item. A pair of red shoes, size nine. Unknown value."

She typed it in, pulled the form from the machine, signed it and gave me a copy. I thanked her.

"Anytime," she said, running her tongue across her orange gloss for my benefit. But her charms were wasted on me.

15

I drove straight over to Mrs. Walbridge's and found her working in her vegetable garden in back of the house. She didn't look glad to see me. She stood with one hand pressed against the small of her back, watching me approach from under a broad straw hat. There was a ribbon around the crown and falling over her shoulder, a faded red, white, and blue stripe that made me wonder if she'd voted for Pickles in the last election. I despised the man and couldn't understand how he got elected year after year. If I lived here I'd try to get him impeached.

The possibility that Arly had done just that and been murdered for it seemed too obvious. The case was too flimsy, too haphazard to be the protecting cocoon of a corrupt lawman. And he didn't look guilty, he looked annoyed. At me and all the trouble I was causing. Maybe it was just that he was a master of mind games and could project innocence as easily as he pulled out his revolver. But I pride myself on being able to read people, to see beyond what they want me to see and catch what they're trying to hide. And I didn't see any guilt lurking behind the sheriff's eyes.

Mrs. Walbridge was wearing sunglasses, which put me at a definite disadvantage. "Frank," she said, her voice trying for patience, "any news?"

I shook my head. "Nothing good. Pickles wouldn't re-open the case. Said there wasn't enough cause."

She turned away and bent over her tomato plants. I watched her crouching there, picking fat, green worms from among the leaves, splitting them and dropping them into a metal pail by her knee. Her fingers moved deftly, as if they didn't need eyes to guide them. I thought to myself that she was a tough old bird, that she'd taken a lot lately and maybe she should decide if Arly was to be avenged.

"Mrs. Walbridge," I began softly, "would you rather I leave it alone?"

Her fingers didn't stop. "No, I wouldn't want that," she said slowly. "It'll just fester if we leave it now."

She picked three worms, splitting them with her thumb-nail and tossing the squirming segments into the bucket. "Them were Sue Toffler's shoes, weren't they?"

"Yes," I said, and waited.

"She hated Arly but it don't make sense she'd do a thing like that. Is it her you suspect?"

I shrugged. "Sue told me she went over there to give Arly hell. They quarreled and she threw her shoes at her. She was so mad she didn't remember them until she got home."

"So that's what she was lookin' for among Arly's things."

"Yes."

She impaled another worm on her yellowed nail. I tried to avoid looking at the writhing mess in her bucket but my eye kept being drawn to the movement. I stepped aside so her body was between me and it. She looked up and grunted. "Don't got no stomach for it, do you, Frank?"

"Guess not," I admitted.

"I never used to neither. But if'n you don't do it, the worms'll take it all." She half-stood, moved her bucket, and waddled a few steps down the row of tomatoes, her fingers searching automatically for more gluttons. "So who then?"

"What about Chad Eby?"

Splat went another worm. "I never liked Chad," she said regretfully. "Thought he'd never amount to nothin' and prob'ly he never will. But he loved Arly, wanted to marry her. She said she wasn't ready and I encouraged that. Maybe if she'd been married, though, none of this would've come about. No, I don't think it was Chad."

I waited and then let it drop. "Not even because she was pregnant?"

Splat, splat. "I don't reckon so," she finally said. "Reckon he could've used that in his favor, to get her to marry him 'n all. If he loved her so much, it don't seem too much to ask, to raise a child maybe not his own."

"What about Pickles then?"

"I been thinkin' on that." Splat. "If I knew what they fought about that night," splat, "it might help."

"I think I know, but it isn't pretty."

"Go on," she coaxed without looking at me.

"He forced himself on her a long time ago. Told her if she said anything, he'd bust How Toffler's pot farm. How being her boyfriend at the time, she kept quiet. The arrangement went on for some time, how long I haven't been able to find out. Arly kept doing it because she didn't want How busted. Then she found out all those years Pickles had been getting a kickback, so it was unlikely he'd bust How anyway. She exploded. Went over to Pickles and gave him a piece of her mind, I imagine. Wasn't much else she could do, the way everyone feels about Pickles around here."

"What do you mean?" she asked in a tired voice.

"I mean in a normal city she could have gone to the DA and pressed charges. I don't know the name for what he did but it's got to be illegal. Blackmail, coercion, wrongful use of authority. And that's beside the statutory rape and kickback scheme. But Chad told me Arly's reputation was so bad no one would believe her anyway. I'm sorry," I stopped myself, too late. "I shouldn't have said that."

"S'all right," she said softly. "I knew my daughter. I knew her doin's with Pickles were wrong. And I knew about all the other men, too. But she wasn't bad, Arly wasn't. And I believe some of the folks in this town would have stood behind her. Even so, it wouldn't have amounted to much. She couldn't have hurt Pickles."

"Why?" I had to keep myself from shouting.

She answered without hesitation. "There's never any trouble in Holler." Splat. "That's what people want from the law. They don't have to like him, they understand him." Splat. "He's from here, his folks were among the first white people in Holler. His daddy and his grand-daddy were the law before him and they learned how to do it. Pickles has some of that left."

"Next you'll tell me you voted for him."

"Weren't no one else on the ballot."

I grimaced in disgust.

"Could be the argument with Pickles didn't have nothin' to do with her dying. Could be it was just a coincidence."

I snorted disbelief. "Yeah, another one. Pickles said it's a coincidence that those shoes were found on the scene. Said someone left them there earlier and Arly went barefoot. And why the hell, excuse me, did Pickles bust How the next day? That's got to be a cover, but of what?"

"Sue Toffler's hatred is at the bottom of this."

I looked at her sharply. "Are you saying you think she did it?"

Mrs. Walbridge shook her head. "No, no, I can't bring myself to think that." Her fingers searched without finding anything. "I don't believe she *could* have. Arly was too strong for her. She could have shot her, yes, but Sue could never strangle Arly. It'd be like sending a kitten in to kill a wild horse."

"What about her husband?"

She sighed and stood up wearily. "I've lived with these people all my life. It's hard to think one of them would take my daughter from me. She was wild, oh I know she was wild, but she had a good heart and people knew that."

She trundled her bucket over to the fence and dumped its slimy contents over. The chickens came eagerly into the sun for their feast and she leaned a minute to watch them.

"Mrs. Walbridge," I said gently, "isn't there anyone you could think of who would want to be rid of her?"

She looked up and her eyes, behind the dark glasses, were shining with pride. "People enjoyed Arly. Some of 'em thought she was crazy but it was the kind of crazy they'd pull my leg about in the A&P. Sometimes it seemed like she was the only thing movin' in this town and people were grateful. Even that spiteful ole Sue Toffler. Her own darn fault if she can't keep her husband home, and she knew it as well as anyone. She just needed Arly to vent her spite on. We're a tight knit group, here in Holler. We need all of us, and every one of us knows it."

I was beginning to wish I'd followed Eby's advice and left it all alone. It was their town, their family, their close knit group that chose to tolerate a killer for the sake of togetherness. If I could just once hear Arly inside me say, 'Yeah, so they said I did myself in, so what?', I might have been able to walk away. But those words would never pass her lips.

"I wish I had something to tell you, Mrs. Walbridge, but I don't. Nothing makes sense; things add up and then turn out to be nothing. I feel like I'm missing one basic fact that would set it all in place, but I can't find it."

"Keep tryin', Frank," she said, sounding like my old friend Eliot.

16

I was hungry to see Baxter, to bury my face in her sweet scent and forget about murder and Holler, Texas. But Eliot used to tell me the point when you're ready to give up is the point to push harder, that the truth is recalcitrant and yields only to persistence. So I drove into town and parked in front of the Department of Public Safety. I found the Office of Records and saw it was Teresa Wains' friend, the heavily made-up vamp, behind the counter. I told her I'd just been to see Teresa, who'd sent me down here to look at the records.

The vamp couldn't have been much over twenty, with a marless complexion beneath her thick warpaint. "I was fixin' to go to lunch," she simped. "But if you know Teresa, I'll just leave you here and you can let yourself out."

She gave me the records I wanted, told me how to lock the door, and closed it after herself. I couldn't believe my luck. Amazing how lubricating a little lie can be. The coroner's report was fat, and I saw the police investigation had been appended onto the end. It was all there, just like Pickles said.

Some boys out fishing had seen her body hanging from the tree. They'd run to Decker's store and spilled their grisly tale. Pickles himself had responded to the call. She'd been pronounced dead at the scene and the body removed for autopsy. She'd died of strangulation. There were rope burns on her neck. Bruises on her arms which were supposed to have been caused by her hitting the tree as she twisted. Her vagina was inflamed and semen had been taken, but I couldn't find any report of its analysis. Under Miscellaneous Notes I found where the sample had been inadvertently destroyed by the lab. Yeah, I bet. Apparently no one had made any effort to find evidence of her assailant, there was no gleaning of possible tissue from under her nails, no search of her clothing for alien fibers. As soon as they'd found the note, her death was labeled suicide and investigation ceased.

The note was there. Three lines, typed double-spaced with no paragraph indentation and an erratic right margin.

> the partyxs over xand i
> founmd the pmonley door i wandt dont
> cry foxr me

That was it. No punctuation or capital letters, no word longer than two syllables. No signature, no motive. It wasn't Arly's, I knew that from my gut. She loved words and if she had ever written a suicide note it more likely would've been a quote from poetry, or at least sounded like one. And it would have contained something personal for her mother. It didn't because whoever had typed this hadn't wanted to think about Mrs. Walbridge and what he was doing to her.

I shuffled through the papers and found the fingerprint report from the typewriter. Only Arly's prints were on the keys; the body of the machine had yielded nothing, as if she'd been wearing gloves when she took it from its case, or it had been wiped clean. All these clues that no one followed up.

I tried to put myself in Pickles' place. If I had found her body and then this note, would I have suspected foul play?

Considering she was a thorn in his side and he was glad to be rid of her, it wasn't totally unnatural that he accepted everything at surface value. That he'd dusted for prints and ordered a semen sample showed he'd given cursory credence to the possibility of homicide. When they were her prints, he'd been satisfied. When the sample had been lost he considered it inconsequential.

Arly had had a lot of lovers, an abundant joy in sex. So she'd made love as her last social act. It wasn't out of character. The suicide was. I've been in journalism long enough to know suicide often does seem out of character at first glance, but in retrospect people usually see clues they didn't notice before. No one I'd talked to had mentioned anything like that.

Pickles had argued with her the day before it happened. Maybe he knew something that led him to accept her suicide. Or maybe he was covering up for someone. Maybe he knew who did it and wanted him free, so he pretended to believe the suicide, glossed over the inconsistencies. The obvious question was: Whose freedom mattered that much to Pickles? And the obvious answer: How Toffler. If How were arrested for murder, Pickles would lose his lucrative kickback.

I left the report on the vamp's desk and locked the door behind me as she'd asked. Then I walked around to the squat jail appended onto the building below Pickles' office. The guy behind the desk was just a kid, probably doing time as a jailer to earn his deputy's badge. I asked to see Howard Toffler.

"He's out at the county camp," he said. "East on 46 about nine miles from town."

"Was he taken directly there or are all prisoners processed through here?" I asked casually.

"They're all processed through here," the kid answered, obviously proud of himself for knowing. "He probably

94

stayed just long enough for his court appearance and when he didn't post bail we sent him out to the camp. These cells are mostly for short-term use."

"When was he arrested?"

"The twenty-third," he said without looking. "I know 'cause I took a couple of days off. When I came in after the weekend he was already out at the camp."

"You're sure?" I asked.

He was displeased at my doubt but looked up the card in the rolodex. "August 23rd, 4:45 P.M., booked and remanded into custody," he crowed.

I thanked him and left. So How was in jail over twenty-four hours before Arly died. The perfect alibi. And it hadn't come from Pickles but from someone who didn't know me from Adam. Another dead end, another good guess that led nowhere.

I had only one more lead and it wasn't nearly as promising as the ones that had failed me. I drove through the blistering heat to the south side of town and pulled into the yard of Armadillo Wreckers. Rod Hauper's Trans Am was parked next to the office, in the only piece of shade. The sun glared off the chrome of rusted autos in various stages of amputation, glinted off the dirt dark with spilled oil, shimmered in heat waves from the tin roof of the office. I stepped inside hoping to find that blessed artificial chill, but all they had was a box fan blowing air out the double doors open to the graveyard of cars in back. Hauper stood behind the counter smoking a cigarette, watching me.

"Howdy, neighbor," he said in the false gusto of commercial enterprise. "Wha'cha need?"

I wiped the sweat off my face with my sleeve. "Looking for a distributor cap for my Celica."

He grinned. "Whyn't you go to Japan? This here's America." And then he guffawed at his humor. "Just kiddin'," he said when I didn't smile. "What kind you want?"

95

"Centrifugal advance with dual points," I bragged, expecting him to be surprised.

His grin didn't flicker. "I knew that wasn't no street machine makin' all that noise. You ever race?"

It occurred to me he might know my modifications by more than sound. Maybe from a little hands on experience. "Only up Lookout Mountain," I deadpanned.

He guffawed again. "That Baxter girl got hot pants, huh? Must come with the territory."

"What do you mean by that?" I hated her name on his tongue.

"Her livin' in Arly's trailer, that's all. Take it easy, man. I din't mean nothin' really."

He'd become instantly conciliatory, hooking his thumbs in his back pockets like he had when I first met him. I felt disgusted and only wanted to get away. "What about that distributor?"

He crouched down behind the counter and rummaged on the shelves. "Hey, whaddaya call a pretty girl in Texas?" he asked, out of sight.

"I don't know," I answered indifferently.

"A Yankee," he barked, popping back up and guffawing again.

I smiled weakly and watched him flick his cigarette out the back door as he walked around to some metal shelving along the wall. As he sorted through the distributors scattered randomly, he laid another one on me. "What's the difference between a '48 Chevy and a girl from Holler?" He looked over his shoulder and I shook my head. "Not everyone's had a '48 Chevy," he chortled.

I chuckled involuntarily, as much at his enjoyment of the jokes as from their humor, and decided he was trying to be nice. It wasn't entirely his fault he was such an asshole. He came back empty-handed. "No go on the distributor," he said. "Sorry, but most folks buy American around here."

That reminded me of the Toyota truck. "You know anyone with a tan and bronze Toy pickup? I've seen it around town."

He shook his head and then shrugged. "Even if you found him and he had an extra cap, it wouldn't fit your car."

"Guess not," I said, and left before he could start another joke.

17

I wanted to head toward the river and Baxter's sweet comfort. But something was edging toward awareness in my mind and it was disturbing enough that I wanted to let it surface, so I nosed my Celica onto the highway and opened the throttle all the way. The hot wind whipped past my face, gritty and full of the smell of farmland decaying in the heat. From the trees along one side of the road a million locusts sang their raspy song, making me shiver as if it were my spine they rubbed their hairy legs against to make that sound.

A hawk was circling above a field to my left and I slowed down to watch his graceful spiral downward and then, when he found nothing, his quick, nearly effortless ascent. I tried to imagine how the pioneers felt, what made them stick it out despite the climate and the inhospital insects, to say nothing of the Indians. It was freedom, of course. Compared to the oppression of civilization, the wild, fierce land beneath a boundless sky had probably felt close to heaven.

Now civilization had come to Texas. Yankees were invading, not to conquer but to find jobs, not to rule but to join the masses in search of economic prosperity. Yankees made me think of Hauper's joke and wonder if his wife was a native or an immigrant. And then I had it, the connection that had been knocking at the door of consciousness: Kerrie Hauper had said How was busted the day after Arly died, not the day before. How did she know? Maybe she was wrong. Or maybe Toffler's perfect alibi had come from Pickles after all, through a falsified arrest report. If that were true, it proved that Pickles thought How did it.

Sue Toffler would know for sure. If I sprang the question right—as an afterthought, a piece of inconsequential information I was asking just to stall for time—I might catch her as surely and surreptitiously as the barb on a hook catches the fish. I remembered a sign Eliot had on the wall of his kitchen, one of those lacquered slabs of wood with letters burned into them that you used to find in tourist stops. "Even a fish wouldn't get caught if he kept his mouth shut." Indeed, I thought. But human fish rarely do, and they're almost always caught. Not through the expertise of the angler, but through the yapping of their own traps. I pointed my old silver steed toward the Toffler place and dug in my spurs.

When I turned into their driveway I cut my engine and coasted under the shade of a giant cottonwood. Her Mustang was in the carport beside How's Ranchero. The only sounds were locusts loud above my head and the whir of the air conditioner chilling the house. I got out and eased the door shut quietly, scanning the yard for the Doberman named Wolf. No sight of him. Still wary, I walked around to the back of the house to see what I could see. I was rewarded by a squad car half-camouflaged behind some bushes. Was Sue playing hanky-panky with a deputy in How's absence, or was it the sheriff himself?

Mindful of the Doberman, I eased up on a window into the living room. At first I had trouble seeing anything in the dim room through the sheer curtain. Then my eye caught movement and I saw Sue pulling her T-shirt off as she stood before a large stuffed rocker. She laughed as she leaned her meager chest toward the chair and I saw a head come out of its depths and Pickles' mouth grasp hungrily for her nipple, his hand kneading her other breast as if he were hoping it would rise like bread.

I noticed something else I hadn't the day she'd stripped for me. Her forearms were bunched with muscles, as if she'd spent a lot of time lifting weights. So maybe Mrs. Walbridge was wrong. A kitten couldn't kill a horse but a wildcat could.

Just then the air conditioner shut off and I saw the Doberman lift its head from the floor by her feet. He was looking right at me. If I made a move his predator eyes would catch the change in patterns outside the window. Or the slightest noise would reach his ears. I didn't relish watching Pickles suckle Sue but I was trapped in place and it was easier than staring at those canine eyes searching for reason to sound alarm. Besides, dogs are good at telepathy and eye contact alone would be enough to rouse him. I stared at Pickles' mouth trying to find sustenance in his skimpy meal, watched Sue's muscles ripple up and down as she leaned on the back of the chair, rocking it gently.

Out of the corner of my eye I saw the Doberman turn to bite a flea in his hindquarters and took the opportunity to duck out of sight. If I could have coasted silently back to the highway I might have left then, but there was no way Wolf would miss my exit. Still, with Pickles there I'd lost my reason for coming. She would corroborate the date on the arrest report and all I'd accomplish would be to set them on guard. Plus they'd know I knew they were cuckolding How while he was in the slammer, something I could maybe use to get him on my side. That set a whole train of thoughts rolling, like whose side How was on. Certainly not theirs.

I slipped around front and rang the doorbell, having no idea what I would say. The Doberman barked as if he'd known of my presence all along. There was a definite note of come-uppance in his voice. Sue took so long to answer the bell I figured Pickles was hiding in the house some-

100

where, and I was right because she finally came alone, with her shirt on. She squinted into the heat with no word of welcome. I decided to come onto her as a ruse, although it wasn't easy to feign attraction to that pinched face. I put my arm across the door in front of her, as if blocking escape, and let my eyes wander lewdly over her body. "Just thought I'd drop by and see if you needed any cheering up," I said, trying to sound suggestive, ignoring the canine growl from behind her.

Her laugh was cruel. "I'm doing just fine."

"I find that hard to believe," I continued, letting my eyes rest on the dollops of breasts beneath the thin cotton shirt. "A woman like you, with her husband gone."

She took that for a compliment and her voice softened. "Some other time. I'm busy today."

I leaned a little closer and traced a line from her earlobe to her collarbone, feeling her melt beneath my touch. Of course she'd already been primed so I didn't give myself all the credit. "Can't I come in? I don't have to stay long."

She laughed deep in her throat and lied easily. "My father-in-law's here."

I stood up, immediately respectful. "Oh. I didn't see a car."

"He flew in," she answered quickly.

I nodded. "He going to get How out?"

"Maybe," she shrugged.

"It must be hard on you, How gone for, what is it, a week now?"

"Something like that," she answered, her eyes narrowing. So I knew I'd been right and she wouldn't even inadvertently contradict Pickles.

"Some other time, then," I half-asked, half-suggested.

"Maybe," she said again, her eyes laughing at me.

I turned to go and she called after me, "Give Baxter my regards." I laughed at her joke but kept moving. From my rear-view mirror I saw her watching from the door, Wolf in front of her now. I saw her kick him and leave him out in the heat for failing in his duty, and I was glad she hadn't let me in. Trading places, with Pickles as the voyeur, was even less appealing than the lady's charms.

18

It was late afternoon by the time I got back to Baxter's. She was sitting at the picnic table under the trees but stood up and walked toward me as I coasted to a stop. I couldn't take my eyes off her body. She was wearing a bikini the color of the Caribbean and her pale Yankee skin was tinged pink from the Texas sun, smooth and taut over her bones. Her breasts were pale moons captured by her top but rippling with her stride. I forced myself to look at her face; the smile I wore took no effort at all.

"Thought you'd be at work," I said, climbing out and trying hard not to touch her naked skin as she lifted her face for a kiss.

"Couldn't," she murmured against my lips. The kiss was casual, as if already habitual. "Too many other things on my mind."

"Such as?" Even her sweat smelled sweet.

She shrugged and led me back to the table in the shade. "For one thing," she began, sitting down across from me and leaning on her elbows so her breasts were cupped nicely in the swimsuit, "I was wondering why you didn't have a job. Are you on vacation or something?"

I laughed in surprise. "I'm AWOL," I admitted. "Supposed to be covering the legislature in Austin."

She nodded. "Aren't they going to be pissed off?"

"Probably," I laughed again, uncomfortable under her inquisition. "Guess I could've called and let Louie know, but Pickles beat me to it."

She raised an eyebrow. "And told him what?"

"That I was raising hell and would they please call me home, something to that effect."

"Could they?"

I looked into her dark eyes, wondering what she wanted to hear. "Depends on how much I want the job."

She digested that a minute. "Sounds like you're not sure."

I shrugged. "Louie would chew me out if I called now, force the issue. I'd rather wait until this is settled and take it from there." Her eyes were really digging into me, seeing something perhaps that I didn't want recognized until I could put a name on it myself. I looked away and saw a crude map drawn on yellow paper on the table. It was weighted down with a rock and fluttering in the wind. "What's this?" I asked, picking it up.

"Chad's map," she answered.

"You thinking about going?"

She shook her head and shrugged at the same time. "That's where he left it."

I studied the pencil lines, the neat printing. "Pickles thinks I'm in with Chad."

"On what?"

"Something to do with Arly. It's not clear."

"How do you know?"

"His tart of a secretary told me. There's a pair for you. A letch and a nympho. She told me Pickles thinks I'm 'in with Chad,' whatever that means."

"Sounds like he's trying to scare you off."

"He doesn't know I heard that. She told me in the hall and then when his door was closed."

"Just because you see her as a tart doesn't mean she's dumb. She's still working for Pickles." There was just a trace of disgust in her voice.

I ignored it. "You think he put her up to it?"

"Doesn't seem if she wanted her job she'd go leaking secrets to stray reporters. Especially ones her boss doesn't like. Why do *you* think she told you?"

"I thought she wanted to get me in bed and was trying to attract my attention."

Baxter laughed in a way I didn't like. "I can see how you would think that."

"What's going on here?" I was smiling but my gut felt queasy.

"Men see women only in sexual terms. That's why we make the best spies."

I bristled. "I don't see women only in sexual terms. You should meet Teresa Wains. She's throwing everything she's got at anything in pants."

"Maybe it's camouflage for what she's really doing," Baxter said, not giving an inch.

"Maybe I could think the same about you," I said coldly, giving her the once-over I'd given Sue Toffler.

"Or I you," she replied.

I took a deep breath. In another minute I'd be storming off in anger and I really didn't want that. "Why do I feel you don't like me all of a sudden?" I asked quietly.

She blushed and leaned back, farther away but her eyes softening, dissolving the anger. "I'm sorry. Sometimes I tend to lump all men together."

"Whose company have I been keeping?"

"Rod Hauper's."

Because I'd just seen him I thought she meant literally, but then I remembered what we were talking about. "What's he done?"

She looked down and I saw her upper lip tremble before she spoke. "Beat the hell out of his wife," she whispered.

"When?"

"This morning."

"Did you hear them?"

"Loud and clear. And then Kerrie came over a few minutes ago, crying. She wanted to know if the bruises would hurt her milk."

"He hit her breasts?" I asked, incredulous.

"Kicked them."

"Jesus." I lowered my head into my hands and tried to listen to the damn grackles. What a town. I wondered how Arly stood it, what with her friendly sheriff and her loving neighbors. I looked up at Baxter. "What did you tell her?"

"I suggested she ask her doctor. She's using the phone now."

"Inside?" I jerked my head at the trailer.

She nodded.

"Why doesn't she leave him?"

"The old story," she said sadly, "no place to go."

"What about her family?"

"Too poor. She's very understanding."

"What about welfare? Won't they set her up?"

"Not unless he deserts her. This isn't exactly a welfare state."

The trailer opened and Kerrie came out with the baby. She was wearing a muu-muu, the bright colors contrasting with how we all felt. I could see she was sore by the way she sort of waddled, as if trying to keep the coarse material away from her skin. Her auburn hair was dirty, pulled away from her face in oily strands and falling heavily down her back. She was so damn small I couldn't understand how any man could lift his hand against her. What could she have done to incite such wrath? The answer, of course, was nothing. It was all Hauper, his meanness, his filth. I remembered how they'd gone to see dirty movies the night Arly died, and how ugly he'd looked when he'd said they'd been too busy to notice anything outside. And I thought if Arly had known what was going on next door it was almost enough to justify her suicide: the whole sick reality of her town.

"Thanks for the phone," Kerrie said, almost sprightly, which made me think at least she had a sympathetic doctor.

"What'd he say?" Baxter asked, solicitous.

"He wants to see me," she said in her little childish voice. "I told him I din't have no car."

"I'll drive you in," Baxter answered immediately.

She looked up and there were tears brimming beneath her pale lashes. "Would you?"

"Sure, let me get dressed." She hurried in to change.

Kerrie sat down on the seat Baxter had just left. I wanted to say something reassuring to her but couldn't think of a blessed thing. And anyway, I reasoned, maybe she'd rather I not know. Though I couldn't see what good that delusion did, when half of Holler knew. She saved me the agony. "How you gettin' along about Arly?" she asked.

I shook my head, the general mood increasing my discouragement. "Not so good," I said, trying to smile.

"She wouldn't want you to give up," she said. "I know because that's what she was always telling me. She said just because I couldn't fix things in my life right now, I shouldn't give up because the time will come when I can."

"Do you believe that?" I asked gently.

She looked down and shifted the baby on her lap. "Not all the time," she answered in her small voice. "But when I remember it, it makes me feel better."

Baxter came out in jeans and a T-shirt, jingling her keys. She came to give me a kiss. "Sorry about before. I'll try to keep my shadows straightened out a little better."

I smiled forgiveness.

"Go on in. There's beer in the fridge."

I nodded. Kerrie had walked to the car and gotten in. I

heard her door close behind us. Still Baxter waited. "What is it?"

"I was just wondering if you'd be here when I got back," she admitted.

"Want to sleep under the stars tonight?"

"Here?"

"By the banks of Purgatory."

"Yeah," she laughed. "I've about had it with Holler."

I nodded. "Me too."

19

We drove through the Texas dusk in silence. The seashell colors tinging the sky were so pretty I guess neither of us wanted to talk about the sordid behavior of the citizens of Holler. We wanted to leave it behind us, in the proverbial dust of our horses' hoofs. Except I had the distinct impression we were going the wrong way. Not that I wanted to go back to Arly's town—for two cents I would have left it to its fate—but the sunset looked so tropical I was reminded of Baxter's bikini; and the thought of spending lazy days on white beaches, swimming in turquoise waters, eating shellfish, sipping rum, making lanquid love beneath the rotary beat of a ceiling fan, was a dream not impossible to realize.

Except we were heading northwest. When we neared the interstate I almost suggested we take it north, to Dallas, where I could quit my job, vacate my apartment, and run away with Baxter to tropical paradise. But when I looked at her in the falling light, she seemed so possessed of her own thoughts that I remembered she had unfinished business too and decided that, after all, I wasn't a kid anymore who could escape responsibility by running off on holiday.

Darkness was settling over the countryside as we climbed the jutting cliffs of the hill country. The limestone rocks stood out like ghosts among the scrubby pines and I remembered Arly; for the first time I cursed her killer not because he'd stolen her but because it fell on me to find him, if only because no one else was interested. Like that other time back home, when everyone had said to let sleeping dogs lie but I couldn't. I'd called it justice then, and that reminded me of how Eby had said I was the Lone Ranger. I couldn't flatter myself that justice was really my motive, but I was at a loss to name it. I surely didn't enjoy wrangling with society's derelicts. Maybe it was just a compulsion for order, the storyteller liking a neat ending, being fascinated by mysteries but unable to accept the unknown. I had to pin down the reality of things because I couldn't tolerate not knowing. I needed to feel in control and as long as mystery existed I felt threatened. If that were true, I would never escape. Because the human mind just can't comprehend it all, and more than one lifetime of mysteries waits to be unraveled.

Baxter's fingers reached across and traced the outline of my ear, brushed my hair back off my neck, and then started to withdraw. I caught and held them in my lap. They lay cool and complacent, and I ran my thumb over the curve of her nails. Sweet Baxter of the porcelain face and smudged eyes, Baxter with her melancholy soul dissected in journals, Baxter giving solace beneath a setting moon. Run away with me, I wanted to say. Let's dig our toes in warm sand, watch sunrise over a turquoise sea, make love beneath a tropical wind. But I didn't say anything. The turnoff for Purgatorio Falls came out of nowhere and I released her hand to downshift. When I was on the road, limestone beneath the rising moon, her hand was gone, and I was thinking of Chad Eby and what he could tell me about Arly's murder.

His map led us to the end of the road, where we left the car and hiked along a narrow path toward the abyss. I could hear the falls in the distance and occasionally a breeze rustled the trees above us; other than that it was silent. All the other campers were down in the civilized area, with running water in the restrooms and picnic tables for their soft behinds. Apparently Texans had had enough of primitive life because Chad's truck had been the only vehicle in the last lot at road's end.

We saw his fire, a small dot in the dark, and then his huddled form crouched over it. He was cooking dinner. The smell of frying fish made me realize I was hungry. I hoped he had enough for company.

"Hey, Chad," I called, when we were still a hundred yards away. I'd seen enough western movies to know you didn't surprise a man in the wilds.

He stood up and watched us come; we had to get close before we could see his smile. He wore a straw cowboy hat with feathers in the brim and a T-shirt with scratchy letters across his chest. His hand hung by his knee, holding a metal spatula catching the firelight. He waved it at us. "Y'all got great timing," he said hospitably. "Just in time for chow."

"Super," Baxter said, making me feel remiss in not feeding her.

"Grab some beer from the cooler," he offered, "and get ready for the best catfish this side of Luisiann."

I decided he probably had no ulterior motive for the invitation, as I'd originally thought. He was so obviously glad for company I realized with a twinge how lonely he must be without Arly. We shook hands like friends. Baxter got the beer and we all hunkered around the fire like good ole boys.

"You catch those?" I asked, watching him flip the filets expertly in the pan.

"Yup. Didn't think I could finish them all, but if you don't eat them fresh you might as well not bother."

Baxter started laughing and I felt a curdle of jealousy that another man could elicit that velvet sound. "I love your shirt," she said between the music.

Chad smiled slowly. "Arly thought it up. We had it done at the state fair in Dallas last year."

"Let me see," I said, unable to read the words.

He stood up and flattened his chest for my benefit. TEXANS DO IT ON BARBED WIRE was printed in the scratchy letters. There were even a few drops of blood dripping off the barbs. I chuckled appreciatively. "That's great," I said. "Sounds like Arly."

"Yeah," he said, crouching back down and poking at the fish. "She was one of a kind."

"Yeah," I said, taking a long draught of beer. He didn't look up and I felt he needed to hear something from me, something true and left unsaid until now. "You know, Arly and me, that was just a holiday romance," I offered softly. "It didn't have much to do with our real lives."

Chad grinned, lifted his hat off and set it on my head as reward. "I knew that," he said, "but I wasn't sure you did."

We ate the most delicious catfish I've ever tasted, along with chunks of crusty french bread, and drank our beer in the pleasant companionship of a campfire encircled by darkness. When the paper plates were curling cinders in the flames, Chad pulled out a doobie and we passed it around like an Indian peacepipe, consecrating our friendship. The drug made my mind lazy, a torpid comfort that carried worries like smoke into the stars.

"Well now," Chad said, stretching his legs out in front of him, "I'm sure you folks didn't drive clear out here because you'd heard about my catfish."

I felt nearly content and didn't want to delve into anything unpleasant so said nothing. Baxter answered, "We'd had enough of civilization."

"Umph," Chad said. "Holler getting to you?"

I came to life. "I can't figure out why Arly stayed there."

He looked at me, squinting as the wind shifted the smoke toward him. "It was home," he said. "She knew her enemies."

"Apparently not well enough," I bit off.

112

"Maybe not." He stood up and dug another beer out of the ice, held it toward me, and tossed it when I nodded. Baxter declined and he got one for himself and settled back in his spot in the dust. "You getting anywhere in your investigation?"

"Nowhere," I said gloomily.

"Maybe it has something to do with her job," Baxter suggested.

Chad shrugged. "I doubt it. She was working in an insurance office, for an old friend of the family who took her on more as a favor to her mother than anything else."

"She must have hated that," I said.

"Not so much. He had a regular secretary and Arly just went in when she wanted and did the typing. She was a whiz typist, you know."

"That's odd. I saw the suicide note in the police report and it was full of typos."

There was a silence and then Baxter said, "Maybe because she was upset."

I shook my head. "There was no punctuation. And the I's weren't capitalized. Seems like that would be automatic to a good typist."

"Maybe it was Freudian," Baxter suggested. "You know, denigrating herself, making herself smaller."

"From what I know of psychology," I argued, "that doesn't follow. The suicidal person is full of himself. Herself."

"What did it say?" Chad asked, not looking at me but staring into the fire.

I thought a minute. "The party's over and I found the only door I want. Don't cry for me."

After a moment he asked, stirring the embers with his stick, "That was it? The whole thing?"

"That was it. Does it sound like Arly?"

"No."

"I didn't think so either."

"So you think someone else typed it?" Baxter asked.

"Yes. Except according to the police report, only her prints were on the keys."

Chad made a sickening sound as the implication sunk in.

Baxter was the one to say it. "That means the killer did it after she was dead, using her hands."

I felt guilty for feeling so elated. "That's what it means," I almost crowed.

Chad stabbed the fire in anger. "As disgusting as that is, it doesn't tell us much, does it?"

"Only that she was murdered," I said. "But not any more about who did it."

"Except he had the sensitivity of a brute," Baxter whispered.

I expelled a long gust of air. "Everything is like that. Fascinating tidbits that lead nowhere."

Baxter led us in another direction. "Mrs. Walbridge said she was political. What was she involved with at the end? Maybe that would help."

"Nothing really," Chad said without hope. "Her latest cause was a home for battered wives. She was trying to scrounge up money from the town but no one was much interested."

"Seems pretty benign." She sounded sad and I knew she was thinking of Kerrie Hauper. Arly had probably been thinking of Kerrie too.

"Was there a need for it in Holler?" I asked.

"Lots of men beat their wives," Chad said. "But I doubt very many of the women would have used the home if Arly had gotten it. That's more a big city thing. Small town folks go to family or neighbors until things cool down."

"Didn't Arly understand that?" I asked.

He shrugged. "I think she felt lost without a cause. And she wanted money from Pickles, felt it was coming to her after what he'd done. She didn't want it for herself, and that seemed a good purpose. She had a fight with him just before it happened, went to him demanding some of his drug profits be put back into the community."

"So that was it." I felt another piece fall into place, inconsequentially. "I knew they'd had an argument but not what it was about."

"That was it," Chad said.

The conversation was getting nowhere. The pieces kept falling into place but they didn't reveal anything. I felt full of beer and excused myself. In the bushes I peed against a tree and tried to sort everything out, tried to find the missing piece, or at least the hole where it should go. Pickles and Sue and How Toffler were all sketched in but they added up to nothing. It all added up to nothing. It was like the sound of the falls coming through the silence; the precipice, the cliff, the pool at the bottom were all unseen, and there was only the sound of motion to tell you something was there. I turned back and saw the glow of campfire through the shrubs, how it silhouetted the leaves with a golden light beside the pitch black. Then a sudden sound pierced the quiet. It came once, a loud flat deadening sound that didn't even echo. I tried to identify it through my groggy mind and then Baxter's scream brought it home as gunfire.

20

Baxter was hiding behind the ice chest, ridiculously, as if its styrofoam rectangle offered any protection. Chad was crumpled by the fire, a dark stain spreading across his shirt. I circled around the clearing, staying in the shrubs and crouching low as I ran, until I was even with Baxter, then I scuttled into the open, grabbed her and pulled her into the bushes with me. Her eyes were huge, her face blanched, her breath coming ragged, interspersed with sobs. I held her close and she clung to me as if I could save her.

"You all right?" I demanded, feeling her body shake in terror.

She nodded against my chest.

"Where did it come from?"

"Don't know," she gasped. "Nowhere. Didn't see. Just Chad jerk, then the noise. He was on the ground. I hid. Oh Frank, I'm such a coward."

"Hush," I said, trying to calm both of us. In the silence, only the fire accompanied the wind. I scanned the dark fringe of forest, seeing nothing. Chad moaned. "Stay here," I told her and crept on hands and knees to where he lay. The blood on his chest wasn't painted on now. It soaked his whole front and I saw that the wound was periously close to his heart. Everything was so still I took a calculated risk that the assailant had gone. "Baxter," I called, and she came, crawling like I had done.

I grabbed the roll of paper towels from his kitchen bag and thrust them at her. "Stuff a wad of these in the wound, try to staunch the bleeding. I'll get the car."

I didn't wait for her assent but ran, still crouched low, down the path to the parking lot. It was empty except for my car and Chad's truck. The truck would have been better but I didn't have his keys so I jumped into my car, kicked the engine into gear, and careened it down the narrow path, hearing stones fly behind me and shrubs being crushed on either side. I sideslid into the clearing and stumbled toward Chad, lifting him as best I could and carrying him to lay him on the back seat. He was still moaning but the sounds were weaker. The wad of paper towels was just gobs of bloody mess now; it had done nothing to stop the flow. Baxter was in the car, pulling his feet from the other side. "Close the door!" I shouted and gunned the engine down the narrow path again, stepping on the accelerator as we hit the pavement, fishtailing a moment in the scattered sand. Then the traction caught and we were barreling through the park toward the ranger's station.

I looked in the rear-view mirror and caught sight of myself beneath Chad's hat. I took it off and tossed it on the empty seat beside me. Baxter was crouched on the floor next to Chad, still trying to stop the blood by holding the torn skin closed with her fingers. The smell was nauseating, a thick humid odor that galled my soul because I knew it was supposed to be mine.

Chad had rewarded me more than he knew when he gave me his hat. The killer had thought it was me left by the campfire while Chad went to the bushes to piss. And he had figured Baxter would be frightened beyond threat, that Chad would be indisposed in the darkness, and I would be an easy target beside the fire. It had all worked, except that it wasn't me and all my instincts said the killer had succeeded, that Chad couldn't survive. But who had known I would be there?

The ranger station was dark. Beyond it a trailer sat under the trees and a light shone from a window. I blasted my horn and swung the car toward the light. Slamming on the brakes, I managed to stop just before I broadsided the fence. The ranger opened the door. "My friend's been shot," I yelled, and watched the anger fall off his face, replaced by alarm. He ran barefoot through the stickers and peered over my shoulder at Chad in the dome light.

"He looks bad," the ranger said. "Follow my jeep."

He had to go back inside for his keys but didn't stop for his boots, and then I knew it really was bad. There was a red light on top of his jeep and a siren and we followed that flashing pulse and wail through the night for what seemed like an eternity. I was vaguely aware of traffic swerving out of our way, pinpricks of worry as we sped through intersections on red lights, but mostly I kept listening for Chad's moans, willing him to hang on.

The hospital was a glare of floodlights. Apparently the ranger had radioed ahead because white uniforms were everywhere waiting for us. They had Chad on a gurney and out of sight while I still leaned on the hood, fighting the nausea that wouldn't go away despite the fresh air, the surcease of bloody stench in the car. Baxter had gone in with him, I'd seen her, as bloody as if she too had been shot, even her face smeared where she'd pushed her hair back. The glare of the hospital door had seared my eyes, and I'd turned away to try and steady my stomach. Slowly I slid down with my back against the car and hung my head between my knees, fighting for control. The world turned black and I pushed myself up to hang my head low, to get the blood into my brain. I thought I was going to lose it completely, and then the world came back and I saw two pale bare feet on the macadam in front of me.

"You better come inside," the ranger said, taking my arm and leading me into the bright hospital, past scurrying uniforms. I saw a trail of blood leading under a closed door and an orderly already mopping it up. Baxter sat against a wall, her head leaned back, her eyes closed. She was covered with blood, her face so pale in the fluorescent light for a minute I thought she was hurt and I lifted my hand weakly toward her, but the ranger's strong arm was leading me another way and I hadn't enough will to resist. He sat me in a chair and I heard a door close, but I just sat staring dazed at the floor. I heard his chair creak as he sat down and I lifted my head, trying to gather my wits.

"You want to tell me what happened?" he asked with gentle authority.

"Don't know," I said thickly. "I went to the bushes to take a leak, heard a shot behind me and then Baxter scream. Somebody shot him, could have been me, I was wearing his hat, I did it by wearing his hat, told him it wasn't important what happened between Arly and me and he gave me his hat. Shouldn't have done it, shouldn't have took it, all my fault." My tongue stopped as my mind realized what I was saying. I had to clear my head, get things straight. "Can I have a drink of water?" I asked hoarsely.

He went out and I leaned my head down between my knees again. I felt so incoherent, my mind just a ball of fuzz with no impulses whatever, just dust and cobwebs. I swore I'd never smoke dope again; nothing was worth losing your coherence. The ranger was gone a long time, or maybe it just seemed long, I couldn't tell. I leaned back and rested my head on the top of the chair, inhaling deeply. There was an awful taste in my mouth, a horrid dread in my mind. What had I said to the ranger? I couldn't remember. Baxter would tell them, I reasoned, but it gave me no relief. I had the hazy impression I'd said something wrong, that my words would be misconstrued. The door opened and I looked up to see Pickles standing there and my throat constricted as if someone had just pulled a noose tight.

He started off with Miranda and my mind reeled. Why the hell was he reciting my rights? "What's going on, Pickles?" I demanded angrily.

"You tell me," he said, smiling.

I wanted to smash that smile back behind his teeth. "I didn't shoot him, I was in the bushes."

"That's where the shot came from."

"Not from where I was," I shouted. "Ask Baxter."

"She doesn't know where the shot came from."

"I didn't do it," I said again, trying to regain control.

"You told the ranger you did."

I shook my head, trying to shake sense into the situation. "No, no, I got confused. It was because of the hat."

"What hat?"

"Chad's hat. He gave it to me and when I went to the bushes, whoever shot him must have thought he was me."

"Who would want to shoot you?"

"You, maybe," I curdled.

He smiled complacently. "I wasn't there. It was just you and Chad and Baxter. Did she do it?"

"Hell no. Neither did I."

"You told the ranger you did."

"He misunderstood. I'm upset, my words came out wrong."

"You're upset because your plan isn't working. You think we're stupid, don'cha? Think because you brought him in we won't suspect you. But you blew it, you stumbled over your own lies."

I stared at him. He was going to frame me. It was convenient, an easy way to get rid of me, to take the pressure off Arly's case. He didn't care who did it, probably didn't even really believe I had done it. But it fit into his plan and he was going to take advantage of it. "You're nuts," I said. "I want a lawyer."

He grinned. "The guilty always do."

"I didn't do it, Pickles," I said, standing up. "I want a lawyer to protect me from you."

"You'll get one, in good time," he said with maddening calm. "Right now I'm charging you with the murder of Chad Eby."

I sank back into my chair and held my head in my hands. TEXANS DO IT ON BARBED WIRE kept going through my head like the refrain of some child's poem. Arly had said it. I could hear her laughing when she'd thought it up, but I didn't feel like laughing. Barbed wire was no joke. It hurt every place it touched you.

21

It was two A.M. before I got my phone call. I hadn't seen
Baxter again; Pickles had taken me out a side door to his
squad car, my hands cuffed behind my back. I was just as
glad Baxter hadn't seen me like that. When we got to the
county jail the same kid I'd seen before booked me and took
my fingerprints. His cheerfulness was irritating and I responded with sullen silence. Then came the hours of interrogation. I still hadn't gotten a drink of water. Chad's blood
was all over me.

The interrogation room was like something out of the
movies, stark with bright fluorescent lights searing my eyes.
I kept waiting for the rubber hoses but the endless questions, the same ones over and over again, were torture
enough. I was exhausted, the muscles in my back ached
from carrying Chad, my whole body was filthy and sore,
and I had to go to the bathroom. But I got no relief. All I
got were questions. Finally the damn cheerful kid came and
led me to the anteroom of the jail and I got to use the
phone. I called Louie.

He was none too happy to be disturbed in his sleep—I
wasn't his favorite person right then anyway—and he
wasn't any help. He chewed me out for being in Holler
when I was supposed to be in Austin covering the legislature. I let him have his say, leaning against the cold wall,

becoming more and more certain he wasn't going to help me.

When he'd run down I said, "Okay, so I'm a bad employee, but I thought we were friends."

"Friends wouldn't let each other down, Frank," he said. "I was counting on you in Austin. I got a boss, too, you know, and he wasn't happy that we got all our Austin stories secondhand. He reminded me that I had picked you, that I'd vouched for you, and you made me look real bad, Frank. Think about that."

"Jeez, I'm sorry I made you look bad, Louie, but they got me on a murder rap down here. That isn't something they slap your wrists over."

"Yeah, well, seems to me you're pretty thick with murder most of the time."

"What's that supposed to mean?"

"How do I know you didn't do it?"

"I'm telling you, Louie, I'm being railroaded."

There was a long silence before he said, "So what do you want?"

"I want the paper to put up bail, let me out so I can find who did do it."

"Why would the paper do that?"

"Because I'm an employee and I was working on a story."

"Not the one assigned to you."

"What the hell," I muttered. "Look, Louie, I only get one phone call. I thought I was calling a friend."

"I don't know any killers."

"You said it. So get me out of here, will you?"

There was another long silence and then he sighed. "I'll do what I can, but I don't think the paper will cover it. And you know, Frank, I'm not sure I can guarantee that you won't skip bail. Maybe you should just sit it out, wait for your trial."

"If I do that I'll never get out. I'm telling you I'm being railroaded. They have no intention of letting me out."

"What the hell were you doing there anyway?" he shouted. "You were supposed to be in Austin covering the legislature."

I'd had enough repetitions that night. "Thanks a whole lot, pal," I said, and hung up.

I sat in the county jail for three days. When no one came to visit I finally asked the guard and he said Pickles left orders for no visitors. When I asked about my lawyer, he said they had to get one from Austin and he would maybe come next week. I was all alone in the cell. I could hear voices down the hall and occasionally a door being unlocked and locked again, but I saw no one but the sour guard who brought my meals. They were practically inedible: cold, reconstituted scrambled eggs, bologna sandwiches on white bread, some glop of a bean stew. When I asked for something to read, I was told library privileges came every two weeks. If I was still there, I could walk down the hall and pick out whatever I wanted. I said what about TV or fresh air and was told they were privileges I had to earn. So I sat. There was no window and the front of my cell opened onto another across the hall, empty. The lights came on at six A.M. and went off at nine. They were bright, showing every crack in the cement walls. I counted them and wished for a baseball to throw, like I'd seen Steve McQueen do in a movie once. I wished for a comic book, a newspaper, *War and Peace,* anything. But most of all I wanted to see Baxter.

I realized she couldn't clear me. What little she knew could be twisted by Pickles into at least not ruling out my guilt. But I wanted to hear her say I didn't do it. I wanted to smell her scent, to feel her lips on mine, to hold her in my arms. Almost as much, I wanted to kill Pickles. The desire was so strong I started to believe I could commit murder as easily as the next guy. And then I rejected that notion. Violence is an easy solution for feeble minds. I was stronger than that; I would triumph through reason. I would win with the law.

On the fourth day they moved me to the county camp. I still hadn't seen a lawyer, but they told me my trial wouldn't come up for months and there was lots of time to get one. I hadn't heard from Louie either, but I'd stifled that hope when bail was set at half a million. At the arraignment they hinted that I'd killed Arly too. There was only one thing good about that: It threw out the suicide verdict. If nothing else, I'd cleared her name.

And finally, on the fifth day, Baxter came. I wasn't in the same category as How Toffler so my visitors saw me inside, separated by a long table with wire mesh between us. We were alone in the room, except for a guard on each side of the divider. I'd never seen anything so beautiful as her face through that screen. She put her fingers to the mesh and I could feel the heat on my hand. I felt like crying.

"You okay?" she asked, her voice like a dream of everything good I'd ever lost.

I nodded, swallowing the lump in my throat. "I gotta get outa here," I whispered hoarsely.

She shook her head, the heavy dark hair brushing her pale cheeks. "It's impossible, Frank. No one can come up with the bail. Mrs. Walbridge tried, she was going to mortgage her house but all she could get was twenty thousand."

I was touched. "Tell her I appreciate that."

"I even called my father," she said, "but all he wanted was for me to come home."

I smiled, her confidence in me giving me courage. "Thanks for trying."

"I wish I could do more. I tried to visit you in Holler but

they wouldn't let me in. I left some books and things. Did you get them?"

I shook my head.

"You look thinner. Aren't you eating?"

"Not much. The food's lousy."

We sat in silence, our fingers touching through the wire. "Did they question you much?" I finally asked.

She shrugged. "All they wanted to hear was that you were gone from the campfire and that I didn't know where the shot came from. I, I really didn't know much. I thought about lying but was afraid I'd only make it worse." She ducked her head, fighting tears.

"You did right," I said. "The truth will come out."

"How, Frank? They're convinced you did it. The paper's blown it up into a triangle between you and Arly and Chad. They make you out to be some Yankee monster, come to disturb the peace of their little town. There was even something about Grand River, how you hounded someone to suicide, a woman named Abby Runnels."

I closed my eyes a second. That meant my mother knew, and I was truly sorry to bring more grief into her life. But at the moment, Baxter was more important to me. "There's some veracity there. I did hound her, but it was for the truth. She committed suicide out of her own guilt."

I saw the struggle behind her eyes to believe me. "You don't lead a very peaceful life, do you?"

"I don't find life peaceful," I said. Once more, as she had when I'd first met her, I saw her give me the benefit of doubt, suspending judgment. It's a rare person who doesn't have to label everything good or bad right off. "I've never killed anyone, Baxter. I may be partly responsible but not through any fault of mine. Whoever killed Chad meant to hit me. I was wearing his hat, remember. When I left for the bushes, they thought it was me by the fire. I bear some weight for that. I went there and exposed him to the killer.

126

But I didn't know it would happen. If I had, I certainly wouldn't have worn his hat. I guess I would've gone, though, and I guess I'm dangerous for that, because I don't stay clear of violence, I follow it like a hound on a scent. Maybe you *should* go home, like your father said."

She shook her head. "I'm involved now. There's something about Arly that's gotten tangled up with me." She ducked her head, then looked at me straight on, "I'll do what I can to help you. I'll see it through."

"There's one thing you can do," I said, wishing I could kiss her.

"Anything," she said, lifting her eyes eagerly.

"Get me a lawyer."

She nodded. "Anything else?"

I could see the guard moving toward us to tell her it was time. "Come back," I said.

She smiled.

I carried that smile back to my bunk, closing my eyes against the glare of lights, trying to keep it alive in my memory. It seemed my only link to survival, to maintaining my sanity in the horror of Holler. Such an ephemeral lifeline, a smile. It wasn't much, but it was all that prevented me from falling into the oblivion of despair.

22

The next day they let me out in the exercise yard. There wasn't much to it: a football field of bare dirt, a couple of basketball hoops without nets, a lattice roof on one side for some shade. There were half a dozen metal picnic tables in the speckled sun and most of the guys were taking advantage of this meager respite from the heat. I'd had enough of sitting so I got a ball from a guard and dribbled it toward one of the hoops. I bounced it around a minute then lofted it and watched it hit the backboard too high. Basketball hadn't been my game, I'd concentrated on track, but I used to enjoy pickup games when I was a kid. I tossed another. It hit the rim and ricocheted off at a crazy angle. It bounced into the shade and one of the guys threw it back. Behind him I saw How Toffler holding court. He saw me too and grinned, his cheeks puffing up into bronze balls, but he didn't break the patter he had going with his cronies.

Sweat was dripping off my chin, staining the ball, making it slippery. My next two shots missed but the third one went in silently and fell through. That made me feel better. I knew everyone was watching me, for lack of anything else moving, and while I didn't want to chum up with them, I didn't want to appear totally inept in their eyes either. So far my fellow inmates had avoided me, feeling me out as to how I'd fit in. I'd heard the usual stories about initiation rites in prison and wasn't eager to butt heads with anyone.

Sooner or later I'd have to, and I hoped by working my muscles I'd have a better chance at resistance.

I'd been playing maybe fifteen minutes and was getting so most of my shots went in. By this time I was drenched and any breeze would have been welcome. But the air was dead. I threw another, it hit the rim and bounced weirdly, and two big brown hands came out from behind me and caught it. How Toffler stood grinning, holding the ball.

"Play ya a game," he said.

"All right," I answered noncommittally.

"Wager a pack of cigarettes."

"I don't smoke."

"A Hershey bar, then. You eat candy, don'cha?"

Sticky chocolate was totally unappealing. "How about a beer?"

"Ain't none in here."

"I don't plan on staying long. Do you?"

"Hell, no," he laughed and started dribbling around me. He was fast for such a big man but I had longer arms and could knock it out of his hands often enough to keep my score ahead of his. He laughed a lot, besides being a smoker, which took his wind. Before long I was so far ahead there wasn't any point in going on. But we did, both of us sweating a river. He stopped laughing, tried hard for a while, then just started funning around, keeping it away from me like a cat with a mouse, letting me have it when I got close and then catching it on the rebound. He gave up making baskets. Finally he caught the ball and held it. "You win," he said generously.

When we stopped the heat really hit me. I would've given anything for a cool pool to dive into, but all they had was a drinking fountain in the sun. Even warm the water tasted good. I drank a long time.

"You'll make yourself sick, drinking like that," he said. "Come on over and sit awhile."

I looked at the guys scattered around the tables. They'd given up watching and gone back to their desultory amusements. "I'm not ready to make friends," I said.

"Over here, then," How said, leading me to a skinny shadow around the building. He put the ball under his ass and sat on it. "Loser's privilege," he said.

I shrugged and crumpled down next to him, drawing my feet in to get them out of the sun.

"Heard you wasted Chad Eby," he said.

"You heard wrong." I closed my eyes against the sun. In the distance the air conditioner on the office kicked in and I hated the guards for having that comfort.

"Somebody said you confessed."

"They twisted my words. Pickles wants to get rid of me, thinks he can get away with this."

"Maybe he can."

I looked up at him a few inches above me. "He gets away with a hell of a lot," I said, thinking of Sue.

"Tit for tat," her husband said, making me laugh. "That wasn't no joke, but I'm glad you still got a sense of humor." He pulled the ball out from under himself and thudded down to my level. "Word is you killed Arly too. Did you?"

"No. Did you?"

He looked at me hard a minute, his dark eyes clouded. "Is that what all your poking around come to, that I did it?"

"Pickles thinks you did."

That got to him. "What makes you think so?"

"He falsified your arrest report, has you in jail a full twenty-four hours before she died when really it was almost twenty-four after."

How didn't take his eyes off mine. "Why would he do that?"

"To protect his kickback on your crop."

His laughter surprised me. "You got him pegged all

right. But I didn't falsify no report, and I got nothing to hide."

"Why would Pickles come to that conclusion?"

"Maybe it's all a smoke screen. Maybe he killed her."

"Why?"

"Why would I?"

"Because she threatened to blow the whistle on him for raping her, removing your protection against getting busted."

"That's ancient history. She knew about his kickback, knew he wouldn't kill a sweet deal. Besides, like I told you before, if she was going to blow the whistle on him she should of done it before she come of age. No jury would believe her now."

"Then what motive would Pickles have?"

"Maybe he was tired of her. Maybe he couldn't shake her and wanted her gone. Maybe he was just sick of the whole thing and took the only door open to him."

I watched him carefully. "Funny, that's the exact phrase in her supposed suicide note."

His eyes got real dark. "Yeah? I wouldn't know. I never seen it."

"Didn't you? Didn't you hold her hands over the keys and pick out that note?"

"Nah. She typed it."

"No, she didn't. Arly was a good typist. The suicide note was full of errors, one a good typist would never make."

"I didn't kill her. Hell, I liked Arly."

"Maybe you liked her too much, loved her even. You couldn't stand sharing her anymore, so you killed her in anger and then tried to cover it up. I'm sure you have a temper, How. Admit you lost it and strangled her."

"It wasn't me, I tell you. I found her that way."

The words hung in the heat like humidity. I squinted up at him. He cast a look sideways to make sure I'd heard him and, finding I had, he looked away, past the barbed wire fence to the horizon. His big hands turned the ball round and round. "I'll deny I ever said that," he finally said.

"All right. No one will take my word against yours in this town. So tell me the rest. Who are you protecting?"

"I ain't protecting nobody."

"You found her dead, typed a phony suicide note, and hung her from a tree for kicks?"

"I didn't hang her. I swear to God."

"What did you do?" When he didn't answer, I prodded, "Come on, How. You can deny anything you say later, but think about this. Somebody's framed us both. Now who would benefit from that if not Pickles?"

"He loses a lot of dough without me," he said, keeping his eyes averted.

"Not if Sue takes your place."

"She wouldn't double-cross me."

"She already has." I watched his head turn real slow and felt his eyes on me like lead. "I paid her a visit last week and Pickles was there."

"Maybe they had things to talk about."

"I saw them, How. I looked through the window and saw her take her shirt off for him. Maybe that's no big deal because she did the same for me, but Pickles had an appetite."

He grunted like I'd hit him in the gut. "That bitch," he muttered. "I did it for her."

"Sue killed her?"

He wiped his arm across his forehead; it came away wet. "I found her bracelet next to Arly. There was a rope around her neck and I figured Sue had surprised her and strangled her from behind. She's stronger than she looks and she hated Arly. I knew she never could of done it if Arly had seen her coming so I figured she must of waited in the trailer for her and then caught her from behind when she wasn't suspecting anything. I was sorry for it. But I thought there was no sense losing both of them. Especially since it'd been done for me, out of love for me. So I thought I'd at least save Sue. I took the rope off, typed the note, and turned on the gas. I left Arly like that, in the trailer. I swear it."

"Didn't you know they always do an autopsy on suicides? And it would prove she died of being strangled, not from the gas?"

"I didn't," he said with so much chagrin I almost believed him. "I figured with the note and all it would be open and shut."

"Who hung her then?"

"I got no idea. That part stumps me."

I let it pass, guessing he was too ashamed to admit the most sordid part of his complicity. "So you did it all to protect Sue?"

"That bitch," he expelled angrily. "I risked my freedom for her. I knew Pickles thought it was me 'cause I'd told him I was pissed off at Arly. She wanted to cut into my crop, said she deserved a percentage 'cause of the protection she'd given early on, when I was getting started."

"Maybe she did," I suggested.

"Yeah. Except she wanted to start some damn home for battered women with it. I knew it wouldn't work. Sooner or later someone would start asking where the funding came from and I'd be busted. But she couldn't see that. I went to Pickles and told him to get her off my back, that she was driving me nuts about it."

"And what did Pickles say?"

"He laughed. Told me when she'd come to him with the same idea he'd slapped her around and it had shut her up. So when she turned up dead, I figured he'd think I took his advice and went too far. And that's what he did think. He went ahead and busted one field and put me in here. The perfect alibi, he said. After Arly's death blew over he was gonna let me out on probation and we'd go on like before. I let him do it, to protect Sue. That bitch. And now she's fucking him. They better laugh now 'cause it won't last long."

"What are you going to do?"

"I'm going to bust this joint and pay them a visit. I hope I catch him with his prick up so I can cut it off."

"Can you get out of here so easily?"

"Hell yes. Nothing to it."

"Take me with you."

The hatred in his eyes might have knocked me down if I hadn't already been in the dust. "Why would I do that?"

"Gratitude, maybe, for telling you the truth. Companionship of a fellow traveler. Why not just an appreciative audience for your humiliation of Pickles?"

The Comanche in him liked that. "Come see me at supper," he grunted, pushing the ball into my chest. "I'll think about it."

23

Security was pretty lax inside the camp, but it didn't seem to facilitate an easy exit and I wondered how How was going to arrange it. All afternoon I had visions of riding out in a laundry truck or scurrying along a secret tunnel. Maybe he could cut the current off part of the fence and we would climb over. As it turned out, none of those devices were necessary. He relied on the oldest trick in the book: he bribed a guard.

The guy's nickname was Squirrel because of his narrow chin and protruding front teeth. He was the main man for getting contraband inside and, of course, How was the main supplier. It cost us six ounces of prime marijuana for a three-hour furlough, long enough for the movies to be shown in the rec room and the half hour of loitering before roll call in our bunks. Six ounces each, and How made no bones about expecting me to come up with my share. That was six hundred dollars I owed him, but since I was bargaining for my freedom and maybe my life I didn't quibble. We made our exit through the plant, a building off limits to inmates that afforded a metal door opening directly onto the employee parking lot.

The lot was well lit and we had to run across the open space and climb a chainlink fence without the cover of darkness. On the other side, the pine forest enveloped us in safety. We stopped and caught our breath, looking back to make sure we hadn't been seen. Then How turned without a word and started trotting through the woods like he knew where he was going, as I supposed he did. He had probably bought his way out more than once and it explained how such a vigorous man could take incarceration with so much calm.

The ground was covered with a thick layer of pine needles and we moved quietly, the pumping of our lungs the noisiest evidence of our passage. I had been trained to run, had even broken a record at my podunk college, and I fell into it with remembered grace. But there was something that went further back than my youth, some primeval memory that made it all familiar: moving through the forest on an urgent mission, men honed to economical traversal of distance, united in purpose beyond the need for words, knowing the other was there by the sound of him, the feel of his presence in the dark. We were one, How and me, warriors on a foray, humans in the forest. I thought of him being Comanche and how I'd read that the Plains Indians were among the most violent cultures known to history, that the qualities they aspired to were courage and the tolerance of pain, and his feet falling easily in the needles were a drumbeat that whispered of a time when what a man was mattered more than it did today, when every moment of his life he was tested and judged, and I felt some of the exhilaration that comes from victory over weakness, your own and your enemies'. I followed him with nostalgia for the time when to be a man was everything.

I also followed with anticipation. I had wanted to come for the most selfish of reasons, vindication. I certainly didn't want to defend Pickles, but I wanted even less to come between these two warlords, and the thought that my justice might be embroiled in How's vengeance was discomforting. He was, after all, Comanche, and he had been duped. He had threatened to castrate Pickles and I wasn't sure his threat had been metaphor or exaggeration. I couldn't be a party to How's revenge; I had to use it for my own purposes. Yet I doubted if I could control him to any degree. I was there by his fiat and I certainly owed him more than Pickles, but I owed most to myself and the possibility of a future beyond Holler, Texas.

Arly's mother had said her town was close-knit, aware of the necessity of each member, supportive of the disparate elements because it could thrive only as a whole. But I couldn't see that this collection of individuals was supportive of anything good; they were like parasites that fed on each other, leeches that sucked the blood of the others' wounds. Some thrived, the gluttons with a taste for pain. Others, like Kerrie Hauper, struggled with disintegration. And some, like Arly, were eliminated because they refused to feed.

It was too easy to blame it all on Texans. They were the quintessential Americans. The harsh environment had created a breed of survivors; that they stood alone in their fight for independence had nurtured belief in the strength of the individual. And though they'd been humiliated in the Civil War and its aftermath of Reconstruction, they'd come into the twentieth century with the great boon of oil, and they'd taken that wealth and power as deriving from their talents when in fact it was an accident of geography. They hated Yankees and greasers, anyone not of them, and forgot that the pioneers who'd wrested Texas from the Indians hadn't stayed but had pushed on westward, continuing their trek away from civilization until they met the great barrier of the Pacific Ocean. Where had they gone then, these men and women who were stifled by neighbors, suppressed by anything but natural law? There was no frontier left to them, hadn't been for a hundred years. I watched How ahead of me, running delicately on his big feet through the forest, and I thought they had been lost in interbreeding, coupling with the sedentary farmers and politicians, subsuming their explorer spirits in a great evolutionary effort to tolerate desk jobs, traffic jams, and the absolute surcease of silence.

How was half German and I thought the regimentation of that cultural inheritance must grapple horribly with the fierce freedom of the Comanche. He had found a niche in society by living outside the law but could survive only within the law's protection. Now he had been duped by his protector and struck an excruciating blow in the seat of his manhood. And it didn't matter that Sue had been unfaithful before; what mattered was that the man who had power over How had taken more than his tribute—he had taken everything. I felt apprehensive in the face of the Comanche's anger.

We came up on his spread from behind, standing in the fringe of the forest to catch our breath and peruse the field of battle from cover. The squad car was in plain view from here, though obscured from the front by brush. How grunted when he saw it, and I wondered if he'd lost the use of English in the heat of his revenge. He gave a long low whistle and waited. Presently the Doberman could be seen coming around the barn, his clipped ears pivoting for his master. How whistled again and the dog bounded to us, silently wagging his tail happily. He was rewarded with a pat on the head, and then sat at his master's feet, awaiting command. I wondered how far the dog's training extended, how much of a weapon he was to How's intent.

The house was dark and we approached it without hiding, making effort only to be quiet. How reached above the side door and extracted a key from a flower pot, carefully inserted it into the lock and turned the tumbler. The door swung into darkness, lit only by the sound of Sue's laughter coming from deep within. I remembered How saying they better laugh now, and I could tell it wasn't an auspicious beginning. I followed his bulk down the hall, wanting to let him go alone but afraid of the consequences. I almost bumped into him in the pitch dark as he stopped at the threshold. Wolf's tail hit my leg and swung into emptiness on the other side, feeling like a drum roll. How switched on the light.

They were sitting in the bed, Sue on Pickles' lap, he within her and his hands on her tits as she leaned back on straight arms. Both their heads swiveled and their eyes blinked in the sudden light, then squinted at their judge and jury. Sue jumped up and pulled the sheet to wrap around herself, backing away from How until she stood cornered against the wall. He advanced on her with slow, deathly accuracy. She looked sick. He pulled the sheet away and threw it to the floor as he raised his hand to hit her, half a dozen times across the mouth. She was crying, yelping with each blow and sinking down against the wall in her nakedness. He let her fall, bending lower to bring the flat of his hand against her face, and when she lay crumpled he gave her a curt kick in the groin, then turned away as if with no intention of ever seeing her again.

Pickles was out of bed. He'd gone for his gun but his holster was buried beneath the pile of clothes and he managed only to get his fingers on the butt before How's foot kicked it across the floor. It thudded against the wallboard a yard from my foot. Wolf looked at it momentarily then lifted excited eyes to his master.

How's fist landed on Pickles' mouth with a crunch of cracking bone. Blood spurted from the ugly orifice and

How kicked again, this time square on the offending private parts, making Pickles crumple like Sue onto the carpet. Even in the heat of the scene I marveled at How's ability to have them both on their knees in less than a minute.

He backed off then, stood in the middle of the room a moment, then grabbed Sue and threw her down next to Pickles, who was holding his genitals and moaning with a face full of blood. With the tenacity of a Comanche he waited until they could handle their pain in silence before he inflicted more, and with the civility of a German the next weapons he chose were words.

"There's no scum lower than you two," he said, his voice thick with rage. "But you're worse than scum, you're stupid scum. Stupid people got no right to live."

"Please, How," Sue sobbed. "Don't kill me."

"Don't kill *you*? What about your lover, don'cha care about him?"

She shook her head violently. "It was nothing, How. Just balling, that's all. I got lonely waiting for you and he was here and your friend and I thought it would be okay. He's just a prick to me, How. I love you, you're the only man I ever wanted, it's just that you weren't here and you know how I am, how I can't wait for anything. Please forgive me, How." She started crawling toward him, sobbing, to cling to his leg.

He suffered her a moment but the look on his face made me want to warn her to get away. I might have if he'd waited a moment longer, but he jerked his foot free and kicked her so hard I heard ribs crack and saw blood spurt from broken skin beneath her breast. The force of the blow sent her sprawling back beside Pickles. She lay tearing at the rug, howling.

Pickles had half risen to his knees. His flabby belly made his cock look ridiculous, shriveled and puny. He spit blood,

140

wiped his hand across his mouth, and searched the room for his gun with fevered eyes. He saw it beyond reach and started wheedling as last resort.

"Come on now, How, you know how it is. It don't mean nothing, wasn't aimed at you. For God's sake, man, show some sense. We're partners. Don't throw that away in anger just because of a little fiddling around. Get some perspective. It's not like she's your virgin daughter or even your unspoiled wife, she's a whore, everyone knows it. Don't throw away our deal over a whore."

"She was my wife," How grumbled from deep in his throat. "I almost gave my life to protect her, I put myself in your goddamn jail for her. But no more, Pickles. We're through. I've had it with your shit."

Even in his fear the words sunk into Pickles' brain. "Whaddaya mean, to protect her?"

"She killed Arly."

We all looked at Sue, who rolled over gasping for air. "I didn't," she screamed.

"I found your goddamn bracelet next to her body," How yelled back. He picked a potted plant off the bureau and threw it at her. The ceramic broke against her knee, spilling dirt and raw roots on her thighs.

She cried out at this new pain. "I didn't," she sobbed, near hysteria. "I must have lost it when I threw my shoes at her. I didn't kill her. I yelled at her and threw my shoes and left, that's all. She was alive when I left."

"Yeah, well, she was dead when I found her, with your bracelet laying right by her head. You hid out in her trailer and strangled her from behind when she wasn't suspecting. The only way you could've done it. She was ten times the woman you are."

She sobbed. "I know you always loved her more, but I didn't kill her. Don't you think I would've told you, don't you know how weak I am and that I could never not tell you something like that? I'd be scared to death if I'd killed her. I'd come to you for help." She started crawling toward him again but he picked up a big perfume bottle and she cringed away. He threw it against the wall, the stain spreading like two pointed legs, dripping a nauseating flowery scent.

"I thought *you* did it," Pickles said, looking back and forth between Sue and How, finally resting his eyes on the man towering over him.

"I know you did, and I let you to protect *her*." How spit the pronoun like it was poison.

Sue sobbed at this fresh attack, then sat up with imploring eyes. "I didn't do it, I was with Pickles that night. Tell him, Pickles, tell him I was with you."

His eyes burned as he evaluated the wisdom of confirming this. "What the hell. She was with me that night, How. I wouldn't tell you that if it weren't true."

How picked another bottle off the bureau and threw it at him, grazing his temple and starting fresh blood flowing. Pickles stumbled to his feet in rage, but How flattened him with a right hook and the sheriff crashed against the wall and stayed there, stupid and helpless.

It was Sue who said it. "If it weren't none of us, then who?"

All eyes shifted to me. In one swift swing I scooped the gun from the floor. The release of the safety thundered in the sudden silence. "You're crazy, all of you," I said. "I'm sorry I ever heard of Holler, Texas, and I'm sure as hell not going to be pinned for your sins."

"Was it you?" How breathed.

I felt gratitude that at least he asked. "No. Do you think I'd be the only one crying murder if I'd done it myself?"

"There's cases like that," Pickles bubbled through the

blood. "Killers so twisted with guilt they can't leave it alone."

"This isn't one of them," I said. "But I'm not going to stick around and rely on Holler justice. Get his cuffs for me, will you, How?"

He calculated. "You couldn't stop me with a slug from that thing. I'd get you before I went down."

I managed a smile. "Probably would. I don't want to shoot you to find out. I just want to secure the sheriff so I can get away. Will you stop me from that?"

How smiled too. "Hell, no." He rummaged in Pickles' uniform and came out with the handcuffs.

"Cuff them to the bed," I said.

He grinned at that, dragged Sue, wailing for mercy, over to the bedstead and pinched one cuff on tight, pulling the chain through the brass rails.

"Now you, Pickles," I said, waving the gun.

"Don't do this, How. You're abetting a criminal, you'll go to prison for this."

"The hell I will," How said. "You're not gonna touch me ever again."

Pickles stood up heavily and limped over beside Sue. "You won't get away, James. There'll be an APB out on you before you've left the county. There's no way you can escape. They're probably already looking for you at the camp. They'll put roadblocks up on every cowpath in Texas."

"Fuck you, Pickles," I said.

"Tough guy, huh? Tough now, wait'll you're gang-banged in prison a few times. You'll change your tune."

How grabbed his wrist, twisted his arm around behind his back and forced him to his knees, locking the cuff and pushing him down on top of Sue. "Go ahead, continue your fun," he growled. "Forget we ever interrupted you." He spit on Sue and walked away, toward the barrel of the gun. "Come on, Frank, let's get out of here."

"After you," I said, still cautious.

He laughed at that, and I could hear from the ease of the sound that most of his wrath was spent. We closed the door on Pickles and Sue and walked through the dark house to the kitchen, where he turned a light on and got two beers from the fridge. "What're you gonna do now, cowboy?" he asked, handing me one.

I drank thirstily, still holding the gun, then grinned at him. "Didn't know you were so prompt at paying your bets."

He laughed. "This time I surprised myself. If I were you, I'd hightail it to Mexico and never come back."

"That's a high price to pay for being innocent."

He watched me over his gurgling bottle as he drank half of it down, then belched. "You got another idea?"

I shook my head. "I've run out of suspects."

"I'm going north," he said, "Canada, Alaska maybe. Why don't you come with me? I like a man can run quiet through the woods. Must be some Indian in your feet."

I appreciated the compliment but didn't relish the company of a man who could hang a friend for any reason. "No thanks," I said, "too cold up there for me."

"Then Mexico's your answer. Or points on south. Hell, there's more territory below the border than above it."

"Maybe. Right now I'd like to borrow a car."

He reached to a board of keyhooks behind him and tossed a ring to me. "Take Sue's Mustang. I bought it for her. When you're through, drive it off a cliff."

"Thanks. You're not going to try and stop me then?"

"What for? I got no reason to help Pickles."

I nodded and, not wanting to lose more time, left How to his own good-byes. The Mustang was in the carport; I

144

turned the engine over and split, with only one look back. Pickles was in that house, mad as a hornet. In a short while he'd be after me and I remembered my jail cell resolution to fight him legally, not with violence. That seemed more difficult than ever with his gun beside me on the seat. I picked it up and, as an act of faith, threw it into the forest as I sped by.

24

So there I was on my way to Mexico. I had wanted a tropical vacation but not like this, not on the run from the law, and not without Baxter. My life wasn't going to be pretty from here on. I had no money, no papers. My credit cards were locked up in the county prison camp; I couldn't have used them anyway because they'd have marked my trail. There was a stash of hundreds hidden under the carpet of my Celica but that was impounded in the police yard. I eased off on the accelerator, realizing that a routine stop for speeding would be the end because I didn't even have a driver's license.

I figured I could sell the car in Piedras Negras, get at most a few hundred for it without the registration. But it was something, maybe enough to hide out in a little village somewhere. I knew the Mexicans would pin me for a criminal and charge exorbitant rates for any help they gave. My future looked grim. Maybe I should stay in the country, find a stray friend who'd moved away from my known stomping grounds and rely on his compassion. I even thought about calling Eliot. But then my heart sank as I saw the gas gauge nudging the red zone. So it was all up. I didn't have money for gas. There was a farmer's lane up ahead, I turned onto it and coasted to a stop in the refuge of darkness.

It galled me to be running when I was innocent. Innocent!

I wanted to scream it at the stars. But they, like the night, were indifferent. It was one of those balmy Texas nights, when the temperature dropped into the livable zone and a light breeze carried the fragrance of farmland. It reminded me of home, and I remembered my grandiose dreams of leaving Grand River for the big time. I'd hurt a lot of people to get where I was, and nothing had come of it. My chance at the big time had turned into a nightmare. I'd walked in cool and high falutin' and proceeded to draw a noose around myself in ignorance. But what was I supposed to do? Let a friend's death be labeled suicide when I knew better? Let Pickles Offut and the whole corpse of Holler rot from natural causes? But then what had I accomplished? I'd succeeded in naming Arly's death murder only to be pinned for the act. And the truth was still elusive. The killer was still free and the way things were going he always would be.

But I wouldn't. Pickles wasn't stupid and I knew he wouldn't be incapacitated forever. Hell, there was probably a phone in the bedroom and even metal beds come apart. He wouldn't move while How was there, but I couldn't count on his hanging around long. I had no one to turn to but Baxter, and I had to move fast. Her trailer would be the first place Pickles looked.

I started the Mustang again, hating the tinny sound of the engine, and backed out the narrow lane onto the blacktop. My best bet would be to call her, have her meet me someplace, hope she could leave before Pickles arrived and tailed her. Disliking it, I nosed the car back toward Holler, knowing I was coming real close to the mouth of a trap. There was no other choice.

I saw a phone booth by a closed gas station and pulled the Mustang around back to conceal it, then walked carefully around the building and watched the road to be sure I was alone. If it was exhilarating to run through the forest with

How, this was pure nauseating fear. Pickles was likely to blow me away on sight, and the convenience to him would more than compensate for any inquiry he'd have to stand up to—which probably wouldn't be much. I had escaped from a murder charge and he thought I was armed. For a flickering instant I regretted throwing his gun away but I banished the regret. If it came to a shoot-out I was lost; even if I got off on the other charges, they'd never let me go after shooting a cop.

I ran around to the booth and smashed the bulb with my hand. I had to let my eyes adjust to the dark before I could see to dial, precious seconds, but I'd felt like a target standing in that shell of light. Then I realized I didn't have the twenty cents to make the call. I cursed my stupidity. I'd lost minutes on a bad plan.

Desperation gripped me now and I ran around to the car and dug the lug wrench out of the trunk. I crept around to the side window of the station and took a quick look for intruders before I smashed it. The burglar alarm went off instantly and I groaned, but there was nothing but to keep going. Reaching inside I unhooked the latch and slid the window open, crawled in and found the phone on the desk. There was a lock on the dial. Cursing, I smashed the wrench on the silver knob and it flew off. The plastic casing cracked in two around the guts, but when I lifted the receiver there was still a dial tone. The alarm was so loud I could barely hear the phone ringing in Baxter's trailer. She picked it up on the third ring.

"Thank God you're home," I almost sobbed.

There was a pause and then she said, "No, I'm not."

My mind reeled. I thought she was telling me to go away but I couldn't give up. "Baxter, I need your help. Everything's blown up in my face."

"Yes," she said, tenderly, but something else quivered beneath the surface.

148

"I'm loose, on the run," I stumbled, confused but pushing on. "I've got to get some money. I hate to ask you but I've got no one else to turn to."

There was silence on her end of the line, and then her words came, carefully measured. "I understand but, listen, my old illness has returned. I'm enjoying a quiet evening home alone." Her voice stressed the words illness and alone. "I'm just fine," she continued, "everything's safe and snug. I don't need you."

The only old illness she'd told me about had been her neurosis, when she'd done everything the opposite of what she'd intended. And then I got it. She wasn't alone, she wasn't safe, and she did need me. "I'm on my way," I said, and hung up.

I climbed back out the window and raced around to the Mustang, gunned the engine and tore out of there. I could hear the burglar alarm a good ways down the road and knew someone would come to investigate. I thought briefly the fact that I'd only used the phone, hadn't rifled the desk for money, would stand in my favor. Nothing would stand in my favor. Pickles believed I'd killed Arly and Chad; witnessing his humiliation would dissolve any doubts in hate. And now the killer was with Baxter. I was sure of it, even though I couldn't fathom why. But if I didn't reach her in time, she would be added to the litany of my guilt. If not for me, Chad would be alive. And now Baxter, sweet melancholy Baxter, brought down because of me. Why had the killer gone after her? What threat was she to him? And who the hell was he?

I reached the intersection with 46 and fishtailed onto the bigger road. This was the dangerous part. It was maybe two miles to the water tower and I was vulnerable all the way. I gunned the engine and tore along the pavement, the injustice of it all curdling in my stomach with fear for Baxter.

The water tower loomed ahead in the moonlight. I almost lost control when I made the turn. Damn loose steering; the car drove like a boat. It shimmied in the ruts, rattled like it'd fall apart beneath my hands. I downshifted to make the turn onto Arly's road and the transmission whined. The generator light came on, flashing red in my face. "Damn piece of shit," I shouted, throwing it into third and flooring it anyway.

Ahead of me a figure walking, wavering in the bouncing headlights. I hoped it was Baxter, escaped. Then I saw the long red hair catching the light, the bundle of baby in a knapsack on her breast. If she hadn't stood in the middle of the road I would've gone by, but she was planted in my path, waving frantically for me to stop. I jammed on the brakes and watched her hobble through the lights to the passenger door. It was locked and I had to reach across and let her in.

Kerrie was crying, the baby whimpering in sympathy. "I hurt my ankle," she sobbed. "I told him how Baxter was my friend, like Arly had been, and he pushed me out of the truck and left me."

The engine had died. I cranked it desperately, not having to ask who had pushed her onto the dark road. The rotors whirred and refused to catch, and then her words sunk in. "What truck?"

In the flashing generator light, she turned her pale bleary eyes to me. "Rod's brother's truck."

"Is it a Toyota?" I yelled.

"Yes," she answered, baffled.

"How long ago?" When she didn't answer I reached across and shook her and the baby started screaming. "How long ago?"

"I don't know. A half hour maybe. I hurt my ankle and couldn't walk."

I cranked the engine once more. It whined and quit and I

gave up. Jerking the handle, I shoved the door open with my shoulder. "Does he have a gun?" I shouted.

She cried in the face of her new abandonment.

"Kerrie, does he have a gun?" I screamed at her.

She shook her head, her eyes wild in the staccato light.

I ran, my feet pounding on the stony pavement, my breath tearing through my lungs. He'd been right under my nose the whole time. My gut wrenched when I thought of going to him for my distributor. No wonder he'd told jokes; he had to have some excuse for laughing in my face. I'd been so stupid. Of course Baxter had told Kerrie we were going camping with Chad. And she had told her husband, never suspecting he'd use the information to commit murder.

I cut through Hauper's place, crashed through the bushes into Arly's yard. The trailer was closed up solid, slivers of light escaping around the drapes. A warning sounded inside my head to slow down, to scope things out, but the thought of Baxter in his filthy hands drove away caution. I lunged at the door, flung it open and barged in.

25

He was on top of her. Her jeans were open and halfway off her hips, her belly pale beneath dark welts where he'd clawed her. I looked to her face and saw the cold glint of a gun at her head, stopping me in my tracks.

Hauper snarled. Then, seeing I was unarmed, "Well, look who's here," he said with sickening control.

He had me and he knew it. I stood helpless with empty fists.

"Come on in, lover boy," the animal said, one leg across Baxter, holding her still, her arms tied behind her back. She jerked up against him.

"Run, Frank," she screamed. "He'll kill you."

He grabbed her hair with his gun hand and banged her head on the floor. "You got that right. I'm gonna kill you both, make it look like a lover's quarrel. Ain't that smart?"

I shook my head. "No, it's dumb, Hauper. You'll never get away with it."

"I got away with all the rest."

I could only hope to stall him. "Got away with what?"

He sniggered. "Rapin' Arly. 'Course I had to quiet her down first. Got her on her hands and knees beggin'. 'Don't hurt me, Rod. Fuck me if you want but don't kick me anymore.' Then when I took her at her word she tried to knee me." He stopped and an ugly smile spread across his face. "I got what I wanted when she couldn't do nothin' about it.

Then someone come along and hung her. And I knew I'd been right 'cause that wouldn't of happened if it hadn't been what she deserved."

I felt sick. "What made you hate her so much?"

"I always hated her. She thought she was too good for me, when she'd fucked every other dude in Holler. Then she started messin' with Kerrie, all that women's lib crap, and I couldn't let her get away with that. 'Course I didn't start out to kill her, just thought the right prick shoved down real deep would set her straight. I did it for her own good but she was so bad nothin' would've helped. When I saw that, I killed her, strangled her with a rope I found layin' by the door. I gave her the lesson anyway, for posterity you might say."

"And then you left her like that?" I breathed, playing desperately for time.

"I put her clothes back on. Covered up her filthy parts, out of consideration for whoever found her. Din't know how much I was helpin' myself 'cause whoever did find her never thought she'd been raped. Still can't figure why they hung her, but I got no complaints."

"How Toffler found her and thought his wife had done it, tried to make it look like suicide to protect Sue."

He giggled in diabolical glee. "Would've worked, too, if you hadn't come nosin' around. You shoudda learned to mind your own business before this. Now it's too late."

"You're sick," I said, hating the sight of his leg on Baxter. She lay still, her eyes burning into me, her mouth a trembling pit of fear.

"No, I ain't. Everythin' I done was right. I know 'cause when I killed Eby I thought I'd made a bad mistake. But instead of me they got you for it. And then I knew I could do anythin' I want. The power of bein' right is on my side. I'll shoot you first, then her. I'll leave the gun in her hand

and they'll think she shot you and then herself. And I'll be clean."

"It's your gun," I reasoned desperately. "They'll trace it to you."

He banged Baxter's head on the floor again. "Tell him whose gun it is."

"It's mine," she sobbed. "I thought you might need it."

Poor Baxter, buying a gun to help me escape. Like everything else, it had turned against us. I took a step toward Hauper.

He threw his other leg over her throat and aimed at my chest. The gun cocking stopped me. If I jumped him, he'd fire. I didn't know if I was as strong as How and if, mortally wounded, I could grapple long enough for Baxter to escape. It seemed the only chance I had. All my selfish manipulations in Grand River had brought me to this and maybe it was my justice. I didn't know about that, but it sure as hell wasn't justice for Baxter. She'd struggled beneath an unearned load all her life, had finally broken free only to be brought down again by my hand. Barbed wire, I thought. Not just Texans but all of us. We all do it in the worst possible way. There was only one shred of an idea left in my mind. "Your story won't wash," I said. "Kerrie knows where we are."

"If a man don't control his wife, he's nothin'. She'll say what I tell her to."

"That ain't your first mistake," Kerrie said, stepping in from the shadows, her baby still in the pouch on her breast. "You didn't kill Arly. I saw her on the road after you'd come home and gone to sleep. But it's too late now. It's enough that you hurt her. I called the cops and they'll get you for killin' Chad."

He stared in disbelief at her mutiny and that instant was my chance. I mimicked How and took a flying leap, kicking the gun from Hauper's hand, following my foot with my body. I heard Baxter cry out and then she was gone and there was only Hauper beneath me, his fists like iron in my face, his knees flailing toward my groin. I beat him to it and came down hard, hearing his breath rush past my ear as I pummeled his stomach until he puked and sputtered vomit. I reached up to turn his head and beat the mess out of his windpipe, wanting him alive to tell his tale to Pickles. When I heard the deep intake of air, I hit him square on the chin and sent him sprawling against the couch, momentarily unconscious.

I crawled over to where Baxter was lying on her side, struggling to gain her knees. "Are you all right?" I asked, tenderly freeing her wrists from the rope.

She nodded, her eyes shiny with fear but alive, alive.

"Help Kerrie," I said, returning to Hauper. He moaned as I threw him on his stomach and secured his hands, tight, behind him. I tied a lot of knots, leaving no chance for him to wriggle loose.

Baxter and Kerrie were crying in each other's arms. I thought of Arly and her feminism and how glad she'd be to see two women comforting each other, and then I heard a siren, as if from another time, wailing in the distance.

26

I was left for hours in one of the sheriff's interrogation rooms, alone. At one point I pounded on the door and demanded attention but was given only coffee and a polite assurance that the sheriff himself would be with me soon. The coffee was reassuring; last time they hadn't even given me water. But I was concerned about Baxter, and worried that after everything I still wouldn't be free. My face was sore, my lip cracked with dried blood, and my body ached with exhaustion. It had been eighteen hours since I'd had any sleep, hours filled with exertion and tension, and even after the coffee I had to work at staying alert.

Finally Pickles came in. He looked as bad as I felt, his mouth swollen and half his face bruised where How had kicked him. I supposed How was halfway to Canada by now, cruising in the freedom I coveted so much. But I was gambling for more, the freedom to leave Holler in broad daylight without a backward glance. Pickles was gruff; I hadn't expected an apology or anything approaching gratitude and I wasn't disappointed. He stood leaning against the closed door, glowering no less hatred at me than he had in Sue's bedroom.

"So you think you're hot stuff," he began, painfully through his puffy lips. "Think you're better at catching criminals than we are."

Since the truth was obvious, I said nothing.

"Well, you're not in the clear yet, mister. You're still a jailbreaker."

I groaned. "You're not going to stick me with that?"

"We'll get there in a minute. First, I want to know a few things. Seems like everybody involved killed Arly, but a person can only be murdered once. She wasn't a cat with nine lives and I don't believe in ghosts. Hauper claimed to kill her but denies the hanging. That means the Comanche did it, trying to protect his wife. That's all clear as far as it goes. Then Kerrie comes up and says she saw Arly on the road that night after everything had already happened. You got any explanation for that?"

I'd thought a lot about Kerrie's statement, and there seemed only one answer. "She cared about Arly," I said, testing it on the lawman, "and she felt responsible for Hauper's going over there in anger. She wanted desperately to know he hadn't hurt her but couldn't bring herself to go knock on the door and ask, afraid of what she'd find. She saw someone else on the road that night, someone who resembled Arly, and she let herself believe it was Arly because she wanted to."

Pickles grunted. "Seems as good an explanation as we're going to get, seeing as the Comanche's gone. Any idea where he lit out to?"

What How had done was gruesome, but Arly was already dead. And the man had done me a good turn; if he hadn't helped me escape, the truth might never have come out. So I lied. "No."

Pickles accepted that. Maybe because he wasn't eager to face him again. That left only me and Sue as witnesses to his humiliation, and she had been just as dirtied. "Next question," he barked. "How'd you get out of the camp?"

I saw no reason to protect Squirrel, so I told him.

157

He nodded. "What're you gonna do now?"

Without hesitation I answered, "I'd like to get as far away from Holler as I can."

It was part of what he wanted to hear. "You gonna write the story for your paper?"

Then I realized I had something to bargain with. "Maybe," I said slowly, "maybe not."

"Tell you what," he smoothed, like an old horse trader, "you give me your word not to print your version of what went down, and I'll drop the jailbreak charge."

I knew what that meant. The local press was in his pocket and all his misdeeds would remain secret. No one would know of the falsified arrest report, his kickback scheme on illegal drugs, his rape of a near child. His reputation would remain untarnished, maybe soiled a little by the explanation for his swollen face, but he wouldn't be drummed from office and probably would get reelected. I was so disgusted with Holler I couldn't bring myself to care much. Like a toad in a cowpie, Pickles and the town seemed made for each other.

"You mean I can walk out of here with no holds whatsoever?"

"The sooner the better," Pickles growled.

I stood up grinning, then winced as the crack in my lip opened and I tasted fresh blood. That Pickles was in worse shape was sweet compensation. "Took a lot to bring us around to wanting the same thing," I observed. "Somehow I think Arly would be pleased."

He grunted. "You know, I lied to you about one thing."

"Just one?" I couldn't resist asking.

He frowned but let it slide. "I do miss her. As much trouble as she was, she was a corker." He smiled and then looked as if the pain it caused made him regret it. "Now get out of here. I don't ever wanna see your face again."

I didn't have to be told twice. But I did turn just outside the door. "Won't you even need me to testify at Hauper's trial?"

The grin on Pickles' face seemed worth every bit of pain this time. "He confessed," he said. "I was in no mood for shenanigans."

I nodded, believing that, and left him to his memories. The cheerful deputy gave me back my wallet and car keys as if I were a guest checking out of a ritzy hotel, and I walked back into the blinding heat. My Celica was parked in a row of squad cars and I liked the look of it, tucked between the vehicles of law and order, and I realized that I'd just given up more than writing Pickles' story; I'd given up journalism all together. If I was going to get bloodied catching killers, from here on out I'd do it for more than glory.

I drove slowly into the traffic, not minding my lack of air-conditioned comfort, not wanting my window closed for anything. The breeze felt too good to stifle. I saw a flower shop up ahead and stopped and bought some roses, in every color they had, then asked directions to the cemetery. The road wound through rolling hills, with limestone crags like sentinels on top. I pulled under the iron gate of Eternal Hope and eased along the narrow alleys, looking for two fresh graves, one a little more sunken than the other. I found them, side by side, beneath a young weeping willow, and left the roses on Arly's name, pulling one red one from the bunch and laying it across Chad Eby's tombstone. If they were there, I hoped they had some comfort in each other.

I climbed back into my silver steed and turned its nose toward Baxter's. Her door was ajar. I opened the screen and stepped inside. Her typewriter and a suitcase were sitting in the middle of the floor, along with a box taped shut.

"I'm back here," she called from the bedroom.

I walked the narrow hall and came upon her pulling the covers off the bed. She looked up and I saw she had bruises on her face. They stood out dark and nasty on her pale cheeks. We stood there a minute, not saying anything, the half-stripped bed between us.

"You leaving?" I asked.

She nodded.

"What about your book?"

"It's finished," she said. "Buried with Arly."

"Where you going?"

She shrugged. "I haven't decided yet."

"Come away with me, Baxter. Let's go be kids together, celebrate being alive."

She looked at me a long time and then she said, "A letter came for you."

"From Dallas?" I asked, thinking it was Louie either firing me or offering a new assignment.

"It's on the table," was all she answered, bending to continue her work.

I found it there, but didn't pick it up right away. It was from Arly and had been returned "address unknown." She'd gotten my street wrong and had typed part of my phone number for the zip. It'd reached Dallas the day after I left, been abandoned in the post office, finally returned as undeliverable. I took it out to the picnic table to read, but let it lay a few moments longer while I listened to the grackles cry above my head. Irritated at my hesitation, I tore the envelope open and spread the typewritten pages out before me.

Dear Frank,

I tried to call you tonight but no answer—just as well, saved you a maudlin phone call. Nothing you could do or say anyway, I've made up my mind. I'm only writing this because I know you'll understand and somehow, after everything, that's important. In spite of everything, because of everything—who the hell knows.

I'm going to kill myself. Don't panic, don't run to the phone or jump in your Celica and come running down here to save me. By the time you get this it'll all be over. I'll be dead and buried. Ha ha. For real.

Don't blame yourself for not being home. I only hope you were out having a good time. Balling some fantastic chick, eating at that French restaurant you always wanted to take me to. Have a meal for me, Frank. Have a drink for me. A fuck, too. I loved all those things. I loved people too, once upon a time. Not any more. Holler has done me in.

I can see you thinking she's drunk, or stoned, or bombed out on Ludes. I can see you reaching for the phone, dialing my number. I can hear it ringing and ringing here in my trailer. Don't bother. I'm going to hang myself from my favorite tree. The rope is right here beside me, a new one I bought for climbing. But I want someone to understand and you understood so much of me that you get to be the lucky guy to get this gutwrenching letter, which will be so when you realize it's true.

This is how it came about. You see, I'm pregnant. No big deal, this day and age, you would think. I would think. My mother doesn't think. She keeps saying how the kid will grow up with a stigma, be a laughing stock because I don't know, can't say for sure, who the father is. I wish it was you but rest assured that's not your fate. You have no fault in this whatsoever. You're only touched by it at all because you touched me, because you were real and good—don't bother denying it. A dying person has a right to her opinions. You are the one I turn to now, the one I choose to understand. Some gift, I know. But be generous and let me give you this. I need to.

You see I have these neighbors. He beats her, all the time. I can hear it clear over here. I've done everything I know to stop him. Have begged her to leave him but she says she has nowhere to go. I even offered my house but she said it wouldn't do any good, he'd just drag her back. I went to our glorious sheriff and he laughed at me. Can you believe it? I got real mad and suggested he use some of his ill-gotten gains to help set up a home for battered women and I truly believe he thought I was crazy. Maybe I am. When I told Chad about it he laughed too. Said maybe I should open a home for unwed mothers. He wants me to get an abortion. Claims to love me and then suggests something like that. There's only one way I'd kill an innocent baby and that's to kill myself along with it. I thought Chad would marry me. He's been after me for months to get married. But he says he doesn't want children and he certainly doesn't want one he doesn't know is his. Says he couldn't live with a little Pickles or a little How or a little who-knows-who growing up under his feet. Some love, huh? Love like that I can live without. That sounds funny now. Love like that I can't live with.

So I'm sitting here in a funk, not knowing what to do. All my friends, so called, have turned on me. Chad doesn't love me unless I commit murder. My mother doesn't love me unless I get a husband, any husband. My sheriff thinks protecting the women of this town is funny, a joke. Ha ha. So here I sit, I'm looking at the paper to see if there's a movie I can stand to watch, something that will take my mind off things for awhile, and I hear Kerrie screaming again. I got up to get a beer, trying to drown my helplessness in numb. But I couldn't. Even though I've tried so many times before, I tried again. The eternal sucker. I put the beer down and ran over there, banged on the door and started yelling that I'd call the cops, that Rod's going to be the one to get his ass kicked. He comes out and grabs me by the hair and drags me, literally, like a caveman, back here. He threw me on the floor and I was so worried about the baby, I just curled around my stomach trying to protect my baby from his kicking, and he raped me. I couldn't do anything to protect myself because I was afraid he'd hurt my baby. But then my instincts came out and at the last minute I couldn't help myself, I brought my knee up hard on his balls. He grabbed my hair and banged my head on the floor and that's the last I remember for a while.

When I woke up I was dressed again and I could hear a typewriter clackity-clackity, real slow. I turned my head and saw How at my table picking out something on my typewriter. I tried to say something but my throat was all tight from where Rod must have choked me and I couldn't make a sound. Then I passed out again. The next time I woke up I smelled this funny odor and I knew right away it was gas. I crawled to the door, pushed it open and rolled out on the ground. I don't know how long I lay there, but after a while I felt stronger and went back inside and turned the oven off and started the air conditioner going with the door open and pretty soon the place cleared out. Then I found what How was typing. A suicide note, for me. Some friend, huh? He was another one who always said he loved me. So he finds me unconscious and he tries to make it look like I did myself in. It doesn't make any sense to me except the camaraderie of the macho male. What else can I think? But I never thought How would take the side of someone like Rod Hauper. I got real sick then. I don't know if it was the gas or the beating Rod gave me, or the knowledge that he raped me—my panties were all sticky so I knew he had—or just the whole sordid town of Holler. I knew then what I wanted to do.

As soon as the air cleared out, I closed the door and sat down at the typewriter. I took How's note out and started writing this. So thoughtful to be provided a suicide note, all neat and tidy. Not exactly what I would write but what difference does it make? No one will care. You watch—no one will grieve much. If they do, it's all pretense because they didn't love me when I was alive. What good does love do a dead person? Not much, I'd say. So when I'm done here, I'll take this down to Decker's store to mail and then come back and do it.

You know the best part? Sue Toffler, How's wife, left me some red shoes to wear. She was over here today, another little parting gift. She was pissed off because How's been around lately and she's jealous. Why be jealous of someone else if your husband isn't faithful? It doesn't have anything to do with me. He loves her, I told her that, but she was real mad and threw her shoes at me and then went off and left them. So I get to wear red shoes on my last walk. I feel like I'm going to my wedding.

Well, that's it, the whole kit and kaboodle. Ugly, ain't it? Don't ever come to Holler. I swear they could make a nun curse God. But I don't. If there is a heaven, me and baby will be there. Maybe not me right away but my baby will. It will never have to know reality.

I want to say something to make you feel better. Don't know what, tho. If you ever do come to Holler, put some flowers on my grave. Happy flowers, all the colors of the rainbow. Like the promise of God's forgiveness. Because that's what I'm counting on now. Bye.

Arly

The wind blew her letter off the table, scattered the pages across her yard, washed them up like driftwood on the beach of her shrubs. I lowered my head on my arms and fought the pain that threatened to swamp me like a tidal wave of grief, remembering how casually I'd decided to stop at that bar that night, how I'd stayed even though I was bored, watching a game on TV between two teams I didn't even like. I'd thought of going home and calling Arly to let her know I was coming. I hadn't because I didn't want anyone waiting for me, I wanted to keep a distance that I could see now was only selfish illusion. The closeness between Arly and me had nothing to do with words. The flowers I'd taken to her grave, the rainbow of roses, had proven that. I wondered what I had that was so precious I would protect it by keeping love away. What could be worth more than a woman laughing in pleasure at the sound of my voice?

164

When I looked up, Baxter was collecting the pages, shoring them against her breast as she retrieved another. The wind lifted the last, threatened to drive it from her, but she caught it as it fluttered high on the breeze, its white face flashing in the sun. Holding it with the others close to her heart, she carried them to me. And it was like Arly, like all the people I'd let down, coming back to give me another chance.